The Shadows of 1915

1915

by

Jerry Burger

Golden Antelope Press
715 E. McPherson
Kirksville, Missouri 63501
2019

ISBN: 978-1-936135-72-1 (1-936135-72-8)

Library of Congress Control Number: 2019943825

Published by:
Golden Antelope Press
715 E. McPherson
Kirksville, Missouri 63501

Available at:
Golden Antelope Press
715 E. McPherson
Kirksville, Missouri, 63501
Phone: (660) 665-0273
http://www.goldenantelope.com
Email: ndelmoni@gmail.com

The Shadows of 1915

Acknowledgements

Telling this story benefitted from the input of dozens of people who provided invaluable feedback along the way. In particular, I thank Carter, Myra and Heather, who graciously read the entire manuscript and shared their usual helpful comments. I also acknowledge Tom Parker for helping me polish the final version of the novel and for providing the encouragement and guidance I needed to become a better writer. And thanks to Betsy and Neal for putting my words into print.

I am grateful to all the members of the Fresno Armenian community who talked with me about that community, particularly those who shared their experiences about living in Armenian Town in the 1950's. Most importantly, I thank the late Berge Bulbulian for writing *The Fresno Armenians* (Word Dancer Press), a priceless resource, and for inviting me into his home one afternoon and answering my seemingly endless stream of questions. Finally, I thank the woman I never met, a survivor of 1915, who in an interview with my wife, then working as a reporter for the *San Jose Mercury News*, told the story of the child she lost, her "little angel," which became the starting point for this novel.

Chapter One

September, 1953
Fresno, California

Mihran Saropian watched from the back seat as rows of headstones eased by and reflected again on how family overrides all other considerations when determining a person's final resting place. His uncle's black Cadillac moved slowly down the white gravel road, penetrating the mid-morning silence as pebbles crunched under heavy tires. Mihran read the familiar inscriptions on the stones they passed. Emerian. Hodoian. Bulbulian. It was the first and most important piece of information about each person buried in the Ararat Cemetery—the family name.

Teresa slid next to him and squeezed his arm. "This really is a cemetery for Armenians only. I thought you were kidding."

"It's been here a long time," Mihran said. "Probably as long as there have been Armenians in Fresno."

"Since 1885," Henry said from the front seat. "We come here every Sunday."

Mihran raised his hands in a what-did-I-tell-you gesture. They were the first words his uncle had spoken since they had started the ride. The other passenger in the car, Mihran's mother, had fallen silent as soon as they entered the cemetery.

Henry pulled the car to the side of the road, and Mihran moved quickly to open the door for his mother. Summer heat radiated from the Cadillac's shiny finish.

"*Sh'norhakal em,*" Tarvez said, using Mihran's extended arm to pull herself from the vehicle. The cemetery was one of the few places she spoke Armenian. She held a glass jar filled with white tea roses.

1

Henry rose from the driver's seat with an audible grunt. He was a large man with round features and thinning hair he combed straight back. His moustache drooped in black and gray streaks on either side of his mouth—a variation of the moustache worn almost uniformly by the older men in the community. He opened the trunk and retrieved the bundle of gold lilies purchased from the stand just outside the front gate of the cemetery. Ohan Minasian, whose arthritic knees had kept him on his stool throughout the transaction, had sold flowers in the same location every weekend and every holiday for as long as Mihran could remember.

Henry handed the flowers and three inexpensive glass vases to Mihran before starting toward the Saropian section with Tarvez. Teresa moved to join them, but Mihran signaled with an open palm that the two of them were to wait here. A breeze from the vineyards surrounding the cemetery brought a moment of relief from the late morning heat and carried with it the sweet odor of drying fruit that permeated the valley this time of year. All around them, row after row of grapes on paper trays were slowly turning into raisins under the early September sun.

"They come here every week?" Teresa asked.

"Just about," Mihran said. "First church, then the cemetery, then, in summer, the picnic. Definitely creatures of habit."

"And how often are you expected to join them?"

"I figure two or three times a year is about right."

Teresa released a soft groan. "Does that schedule include fiancés?"

"Probably."

"Another reason to keep things quiet."

Mihran nodded. It had been Teresa's idea to keep their engagement, now only two weeks old, a secret. He did not understand her reservations, but he had recognized for some time that there was a tentative and guarded part to Teresa that he did not yet have access to.

They made their way to a nearby water faucet, mercifully located in the shade of an expansive oak. It was not yet noon, and their clothes were already sticking to their damp skin. Mihran filled the vases while Teresa surveyed the acres of well-kept lawn.

"What's with the fancy car?" Teresa asked.

"That's just Uncle Henry. He gets a new one every year."

"Always a Cadillac?"

"Always."

"To show off?"

"More like making a statement."

"I'm still not sure why you thought I needed to see this."

Mihran finished arranging the lilies in the vases and joined her. They watched from a distance as Henry and Tarvez lowered their heads in front of the Saropian stones. Watery pools of heat rose from a single strip of black asphalt that cut through the heart of the cemetery. The scent of newly mown grass lingered in the heavy air.

Mihran glanced to his right and was not surprised to see Eddie Hokokian standing in the middle of the Hokokian tombstones. Eddie had been crushed under a collapsing stack of fertilizer drums one week before he would have started high school. As always, he wore the blue denim overalls he was killed in. Not far away, Mihran spied Jivan Margosian. His father's best friend and the man who taught Mihran to play blackjack. Lung cancer. And eight-year-old Ruth Ann Sarkisian, whose family had lived on K Street just behind the Saropians. Polio. Today she was skipping rope.

"Do you believe in ghosts?" Mihran asked.

"You mean like Halloween ghosts?" Teresa said. "Like *boo*?"

"Something a little more sophisticated."

"Like Marley's ghost?"

"Sort of."

"Spirits who come back from the afterlife?" Teresa said. "I can't say I put a lot of stock in that sort of thing."

"The old Armenians talk about it a lot," Mihran said. "They say if the deceased is not ready to leave this world, then his soul—or part of it—stays behind."

"Is that why you brought me here?" Teresa asked. "To tell me that my fiancé—a college student no less—sees ghosts?"

Mihran shrugged. "It's part of the culture."

"And where do these reluctant souls hang out?"

"Anywhere they want to, I guess. But you certainly could find some around here."

A rickety flatbed truck clattered past the entrance to the cemetery and slowed as it reached the edge of a neighboring vineyard. The truck, its grill orange with rust, kicked up a cloud of dust as it came to a stop. More than a dozen workers climbed out of the back. With little conversation, they placed cloth hats on their heads and moved in single-file lines down the rows. Children carrying metal pails and rolls of brown paper were included in the procession. Wooden frames the men hooked over their shoulders provided a rhythmic clicking as the workers prepared to pick the owner's grapes.

"So why don't these ghosts just go on to heaven or wherever?" Teresa asked. "What are they waiting for?"

"The way the elders tell it," Mihran said, "the spirits need to know that what they started in life is finished. They're kind of waiting to see how things turn out. To make sure the life they lived had a purpose."

"And the elders see these ghosts?"

"A few claim to. But most of the time it's a cousin or a neighbor who swears they saw a dead relative wandering through an orchard or sitting at the dinner table."

"Maybe the ghosts only exist in the minds of the perceivers," Teresa said. "Maybe it's the living who need to make sense of every life."

"Could be," Mihran said. "But would that make them any less real?"

The sound of pickers dropping metal pails and arranging wooden frames trickled through the warm summer air. Mihran watched as Henry and Tarvez made their way from the Saropian section to a nearby collection of stones. It was the next step in the Sunday routine—paying respect to lost friends.

"Come on." Mihran retrieved the vases of flowers. "I want to make some introductions."

As always, the grass in the Saropian section was especially green and recently clipped. Each of the five flat stones surrounding the family marker had been cleared of dirt and debris, the result, Mihran knew, of his uncle leaving a little money for the grounds keepers. The family marker featured a floral border and raised letters and was among the largest and most visible in the cemetery. Henry had selected it himself. The Saropians had enough space, his uncle liked to say, for four and possibly five generations.

Mihran placed each vase in its proper location then held Teresa's hand while the two of them stood quietly in front of the stones for a respectful minute.

"Sirak and Ana Saropian." Mihran pointed to the two middle stones. "My grandparents. Came over from the old country. I never met him, and she died when I was too young to remember."

He gestured toward the stone to their left. The most ornate of the group, etched with images of flowers and bold letters. "Katarine. Henry's wife. Died two years ago from breast cancer. She was 57."

"Too young," Teresa said.

Mihran stepped to the grave just to the right of the family marker and paused.

"Bedros Saropian, my father." Scattered images from the funeral floated through his awareness. Dark coats and umbrellas on a dismal winter day.

Teresa fell silent. As Mihran had hoped, she seemed as susceptible to the emotional call of this place as he was.

"There's one more," Mihran said.

The last stone, smaller than the others, was adorned with the tea roses Tarvez had carried that morning. Mihran waited for Teresa to read the inscription.

Vartouhi Mariam Artinian
April 12, 1915 - August 1915
"Lost Angel"

"Uncle Henry had it made last year," Mihran said. "For my mother."

"Who's Vartouhi?" Teresa asked.

"My sister."

Teresa raised an eyebrow.

"*This* is why I brought you here," Mihran said. "I've got a story to tell you. It's the family's story. And if you're going to be part of the family, it becomes your story as well."

August, 1915
The Plains of Armenia

Their feet, swollen and blistered from three days of walking, pushed forward on the dry soil, sending up clouds of dust to sting their eyes and coat their skin with reddish-brown dirt. Tarvez kept one hand over her baby's eyes. The other held her daughter tightly to her chest despite the heat. Only her child, she reminded herself. Above all else, she must protect Vartouhi.

More than a thousand people from her vilayet had started the march. The caravan had stretched for more than a mile, slumped-shouldered women and children and a few frail men moving in step through the expansive Armenian grasslands under an immense sky. Some of the women pushed wooden carts. A few from the wealthier families used donkeys to transport their belongings. But most carried their possessions in the pockets of their overdresses and in cloth sacks strapped across their backs. Turkish gendarmes in tattered and stained uniforms rode on horseback at both ends of the procession.

The gendarmes led them away from the main roads to craggy trails marked by water-carved furrows and scattered boulders. The vast openness of the land was unfamiliar to Tarvez, who had traveled outside her village only twice in her 22 years, both trips to see relatives who lived in the higher lands to the east. The first few days the caravan had passed stands of oaks, an occasional pomegranate tree, and patches of purple rhododendrons that reminded Tarvez of the flowers outside her home. But now she could see only a few trees scattered across the horizon, and they had passed no other travelers all morning.

At mid-day, Anig Erganian, 71 years old last Christmas, dropped to her knees.

"Bring water," someone called out.

"She must have shade," another woman said, glancing upward. The morning clouds had given way to a penetrating sun. "This is too much for an old woman."

Razmouhi Erganian cupped her mother's elbow. "Mayr, we must continue."

But Anig only lowered her shoulders and shifted her weight until she appeared to be kneeling in prayer.

The gendarme was upon them at once. The Turk cracked his whip from atop his horse and ordered the women to continue. Razmouhi tugged on her mother's arm, pleading with her to stand. But the old woman only lowered her chin.

"I will join you later," Anig said, her eyes facing the ground. "When I have had a chance to rest."

That evening, after a dinner of flat bread and salted lamb, Tarvez and her cousin Sona arranged their possessions beside a small stand of trees.

"The trees will protect us from the night winds," Sona said.

Tarvez raked the dry soil with her fingers then ground the broken clumps with her knuckles until the earth was reduced to a soft powder. She removed the shawl from around her head and laid it on the prepared surface. Sona used the edge of her palm to smooth the cloth from the center outward until it resembled the bed the children slept in at home.

Tarvez laid her child on the white cotton shawl, and Sona placed her own son beside Vartouhi. Arakel had been born two weeks before Tarvez' daughter. To thwart evil spirits, the two women had spent most of their pregnancies together. The alk, *the family elders had reasoned, would not take an unborn baby as long as another woman with child was nearby. So Sona and Tarvez had worked the same chores throughout the winter and spring. The cousins often stood side-by-side while tending goats and sheep and comparing the changes in their bodies. Both godmothers had correctly predicted a boy for Sona and a girl for Tarvez. To Tarvez, it was almost as if Arakel were her own child. She had even nursed the boy for several days when Sona was bedridden with fever.*

Razmouhi Erganian was among the group who shared a fire with the cousins that night. She spent much of the meal staring down the road in the direction where her mother had stopped to rest.

"Mayr will be here soon," Razmouhi said as the women prepared to sleep. She leaned against a large boulder, a location
that allowed an open view of the moonlit road. "I've saved
her some supper. She will be hungry."

Tarvez and Sona positioned themselves on either side of their
babies. Sona fell asleep instantly, while Tarvez pressed her
nose and mouth against Vartouhi's cheek and hummed a soft
lullaby to her already-sleeping child. Tarvez was afraid to
close her eyes. She survived the days by concentrating on her
daughter, clinging to a belief that if she protected Vartouhi,
God would protect the rest of her family and her people. But
at night, when her baby was asleep and the clamor of the
day faded, the thoughts she feared the most made themselves
known. How much longer must they travel? What would her
home look like when they returned? And what had happened
to her husband? She began to doze, but her sleep was invaded
by the image of a hundred Turkish soldiers roaring through
her vilayet. Once again she heard the sound of shattering
glass and the explosion of gunfire.

Tarvez rolled onto her back, seeking reassurance in a silent
prayer. She stared into the endless sky and listened to the
sounds of the night while she gradually surrendered to her
exhaustion. Wind surging in gusts and the scraping of horse
hoofs mimicked voices. Soon she heard the crackling of flames
and breathed in the acrid odor of burning wood. She saw
seven-year-old Deran Halebian race down the center of the
road, just as he had three nights earlier.

"What is burning?" Tarvez once again yelled to the boy.

"Stores," Deran said, bending at the waist to catch his breath.
"The grocery and the bakery."

"There are three fires," Tarvez said. "What else?"

"The church." The boy was running again. "They're burning
the Apostolic Church."

Tarvez was awakened by Vartouhi's soft whimper. She fed
her child in the privacy afforded by the predawn darkness.
In the first gray traces of morning light, she saw Razmouhi

still sitting against the boulder staring down the empty road. Uneaten slices of bread and lamb rested in her lap.

***

When they reached the mountains later that day, the gendarmes ordered all carts and donkeys abandoned. Possessions that could not be carried would be left behind. Murmurs of protest spread among the women. The carts were filled with bread, beans, dried fruit and grain, and, as was the tradition of the Armenian people, the owners had shared the contents with the entire vilayet. The women stuffed their shawls and pockets with as much food as they could hold. Blankets, clothing and prized family possessions like dishes and carpets were left along the roadside. The donkeys wandered free.

The mountain road soon became a narrow trail lined with scraggly brush that scraped and cut the women's legs. The children, some wearing cloth shoes, cried and complained. Many of the elderly found the climb impossible. Tarvez prayed for God to give them all the strength to continue. Although she knew it was selfish, she also asked that he especially protect her husband Kevork.

At first, Tarvez had been proud of the way Kevork responded to the proclamations nailed to walls and posts around the vilayet. All Armenians and Christians were being relocated. A result of the changing situation in the war with Russia. They would return to their homes when it was safe. Tarvez watched from the back of the crowd as her husband stood on the steps of the Apostolic Church, side by side with the priest, encouraging the gathering of men to act as one. Although only 24, Kevork had gained a level of respect among the men in the community. His resonant voice added a sense of certainty to his words. Tarvez could not have been happier the day her parents informed her of their choice for her husband.

But when the Turkish authorities came, Kevork was among the first arrested. They arrived as the family was sitting down for their evening meal. Two policemen and three soldiers.

*The tallest of the police officers called out from the doorway.
"Kevork Artinian."*

*The other men in the Artinian home rose, but Kevork would
not acknowledge the intruders. He remained seated on the
floor and stared into Tarvez' eyes. Just before the soldiers
pinned his arms behind him and pressed his face into the meal
he had not yet started, Kevork leaned forward and whispered
to his wife.*

*"I will return," he said with such uncompromising confidence
that she had no choice but to believe him.*

***

*When the caravan reached the craggy rocks near the top of the
first ridge, the women came across a body lying in the middle of the road. Each marcher stopped when she reached the
corpse, and soon a band of women circled the deceased. Children were kept away. The dead woman's billowing overdress
identified her as Armenian, but the face was unrecognizably
swollen and distorted from the summer sun.*

"She is from another vilayet," *Ovsanna said.*

*"At the very least, we must give her a Christian burial," some-
one added.*

*Suggestions for how to proceed were passed among the women.
But the plans were cut short when a gendarme rode through
the middle of the group.*

*"We have no time to worry about one dead woman," he yelled.
"Let the scavengers take care of her."*

*The women slowly returned to their place in line, most glanc-
ing back once or twice as if to apologize for abandoning the
deceased. The march proceeded in silence.*

*"She was very old," Ovsanna said to Tarvez long after the
corpse was out of view. "Most likely, she was ill before."*

*No more than an hour later, they came upon six more bodies
lying on a patch of dried grass by the side of the road. This*

time the gendarme positioned his horse next to the corpses to keep the women from stopping. Tarvez told herself to not look, but her eyes were drawn to the scene as she passed. Five women and one girl with braids in her hair. All wearing traditional Armenian overdresses. They were arranged in a circle, each woman lying with her head near the next woman's feet. The girl was curled up in the center. Strangely, images of purple rhododendrons came to mind. But before she could consider her reaction, a light breeze swept the rancid odor of decaying flesh into Tarvez' face, causing her throat to close up and her stomach to churn. She turned away, gulping air as she suppressed the reflex and cupped a hand over her daughter's nose and mouth.

That night they camped on the banks of a small river. The women lined both sides of the river, washing the earth from their arms and faces and bathing their children in the cool water. They filled bottles and jars for their evening meal and for the next day's journey. Tarvez scooped handsful of water onto her daughter and then into her own mouth. She allowed the sweet metallic taste to linger on her tongue. But she could not wash away the odor of the decaying corpses that had stayed with her all afternoon. Nor could she eliminate the thoughts the discovery had evoked. Except for the oldest men and the boys not yet showing signs of manhood, every male in her vilayet had been taken away. The missing included Kevork's two brothers and his sixty-year-old father. Rumors nourished by fear had spread among the women. Araxi, whose husband and fourteen-year-old son had been arrested, insisted that the men were merely being questioned. Once the Turks determined that there were no traitors among them, she said, everyone will be released. But Zabel Derderian, the grocer's wife who spoke often with traveling merchants and farmers from other regions, told stories about events in Van and Urfa.

"It's happening everywhere," she said. "First they put our sons in their army. Then they take the men. Who is left to stop them?"

The women had gathered outside the government building the morning after the arrests until the police captain appeared on

*the steps and ordered them to go home. They would be re-
united with their husbands in due time. They had three days
to prepare for the relocation.*

***

*The heat intensified as soon as they crested the highest ridge.
Except for a few white wisps resting on the horizon, the clouds
that had at times protected them from the sun were gone. The
distance between marchers grew as the heat bore down on
them and the women struggled to keep their balance on the
steep decline. Scratches on Tarvez' arms stung with dust and
perspiration, and the straps from her cloth sack cut into her
shoulder. She shifted Vartouhi from one arm to the other to
relieve the pain in her increasingly weak limbs. Heat radiating
from the dry earth penetrated the soles of her shoes.*

*The women no longer prayed aloud or recited scripture. Now
talking only left their mouths dry. A child marching behind Tarvez gave out a soft high-pitched moan with each
step. When she became aware that the moaning had stopped,
Tarvez turned to find only a line of women without children.
Later that day, with the sun perched directly overhead, she
passed an older woman she recognized as the tailor's wife.
The woman sat on the side of the road with her hands resting
in her lap. Strands of gray hair fell across the sides of her
face where her scarf had come undone. Tarvez paused to offer help, but the look of resignation in the woman's eyes told
her to move on. Few of the elderly had made it this far.*

In the late afternoon, Tarvez' cousin stepped beside her.

*"Those trees," Sona said. "Do they seem like a fitting resting
place?"*

*Up ahead, a small stand of dead trees cast leafless shadows
across the trail.*

"You know we are not allowed to stop," Tarvez said.

Sona paused a long moment before replying.

"For my boy," she said. "For Arakel."

Tarvez studied the baby. Arakel's limbs dangled loosely in Sona's arms, and his head drooped to the side at an odd angle. Tarvez felt her heart pound once in her chest, and then it seemed to stop beating altogether. She placed a hand across the boy's cheek and felt the lifeless skin. Tarvez met her cousin's eye, and Sona acknowledged the fact with an almost imperceptible nod.

The women wrapped Arakel in the shawl Tarvez had been using to protect her face and neck from the sun. The cloth was stained with perspiration and dust, but it was as close to white linen as they could manage, and the women hoped the angel of death would find it sufficiently pure to accept Arakel's soul. Sona gently placed her son against the base of the tallest tree.

Mindful of the approaching gendarme, Tarvez said a short prayer. "One day we will place a stone for Arakel next to the other Artinian stones," she told her cousin.

"When we return, the family will share a hokeh hatz *meal," Sona said. "And the priest will pray for Arakel. When we return."*

Tarvez pressed her own child against her chest. She tapped lightly on Vartouhi's back until her daughter responded with a deep breath and a whimper.

***

They camped along a ridge of sharp rocks that night, the first time they had not stopped near water. The still air that accompanied the onset of darkness provided no relief from the heat. Tarvez dabbed her daughter's lips with a few drops from her last jar of water. While the women prepared their meals and mothers attended to their children, Sona sat quietly by herself atop a large boulder, gazing back at the mountains.

Ovsanna unfolded pieces of flat bread from her scarf and handed them to Tarvez. "Your cousin," she said, glancing toward Sona and then to the baby in Tarvez' arms.

"She will join us soon," Tarvez said. She placed the bread into a copper bowl she pulled from her possessions.

"We have been walking so many days," Ovsanna said. "We should be there by now. We were supposed to be there by now."

Tarvez opened a small cloth bag of dried figs. She glanced at her cousin when she knew Ovsanna was not looking. Sona, silhouetted in the last of the day's light, seemed far away and unreachable.

"We are traveling so slow." Ovsanna set a small bottle of water next to the food. "The men will get to the relocation before we do. Who will make their houses and prepare their meals? Sarkis will be helpless without me."

Tarvez set the figs in the bowl next to the bread. She started to add some dried mulberries but decided to save them for another meal.

"I hope the soil is good." Ovsanna glanced about as if survey-ing the land. "We still have time to plant greens and squash. And we will need some blankets for winter, if we are gone that long. I hope the church is large and beautiful. I think it will be beautiful, with old wood and a golden cross. And we will need chickens, and cows for milk and cheese. Sarkis would eat cheese with every meal if he could."

Tarvez placed the tips of her fingers lightly on the back of her friend's hand. Ovsanna became instantly quiet. They listened to the crackling of a nearby fire for several minutes before continuing their evening meal in silence.

Just as the women and children were finishing their meager dinners, dozens of Turkish soldiers on horseback thundered into their camp brandishing bayonets and chanting military slogans. The gendarmes watched with disinterest as the invad-ing soldiers tore open the women's bags and helped themselves to what remained of their possessions.

Tarvez scooped up Vartouhi and moved away from the fire and toward the shelter of darkness. But a short, stocky soldier grabbed her from behind and threw her to the ground. Tarvez wrapped both arms around her daughter as the Turk leaned over them. His thin moustache glistened with perspiration, and he reeked of burnt leather and rotting meat. The soldier thrust his hands into the pockets of Tarvez's overdress. When she pulled away, he ripped the pockets open, spilling precious pieces of food to the ground. The Turk seemed delighted by the sight. He stomped the dried mulberries and bread, then kicked everything to the side in a spray of dust and dirt.

Tarvez pushed herself to her feet, but the soldier grabbed her necklace. The silver cross and chain Kevork had given her on their wedding day.

"Tell your Christian God to protect you now," he said.

He ripped the cross from her throat. The chain sliced through Tarvez' skin before snapping. She pressed Vartouhi to her chest. Drops of blood fell on the baby's head.

The women huddled in groups, pushing their children to the center of the circles.

"Virgins," the soldiers yelled. "We want your virgins."

Alik Donoyan knelt on the ground next to Tarvez, her body wrapped around her daughter, Maro, a thin girl no older than 14. A broad-chested soldier with black stains across the front of his uniform pushed Alik to the ground with the heel of his boot. He lifted Maro with little effort and tossed her to two other soldiers who tore the overdress and long silk pants from the girl's body. Alik ran toward her daughter but was knocked to the ground by the butt-end of a soldier's rifle.

The attackers cheered each time a girl was pulled from the huddles. They sang and chanted. The soldiers smacked the women's backs with sticks and open palms, then pulled them from their huddles and stripped them of their clothes. They tossed pieces of torn clothing into a large pile, doused the clothes and the last of the women's possessions with kerosene, and lit a fire.

***

*The next day, they descended into the heat of the desert.
The women wrapped the few scraps of cloth they could find
around their feet to withstand the burning sand. Tarvez used
strips torn from the sack she had carried to shield Vartouhi
from the sun. But there was not enough material to cover the
women's bodies, and they avoided looking at one another to
lessen the collective shame of their nakedness. Soon blisters
formed where clothing once protected skin from sun. Each of
the girls abducted the previous night had become eerily quiet.
Some hid their faces in their hands, while others stared straight
ahead with expressionless gazes. Although the women knew
the girls had been violated, no one said so aloud.*

*The soldiers had left them without food and water. A few
women had eaten blades of grass pulled from patches alongside the road. But now that they had reached the desert, there
was no grass to be found. Tarvez had tried to feed Vartouhi,
but her body had little nourishment to offer. They marched all
morning without water. Tarvez became dizzy and her tongue
started to swell. A low hum filled her ears. The edges of her
vision darkened. She concentrated on each step. She and her
child would not be left behind.*

*The humming in Tarvez' ears became a roar, and it was not
until the women in front of her stopped that she realized it was
the rush of water she was hearing. The women stumbled their
way over a line of sharp rocks and stood on a shallow ridge
overlooking the river. Tarvez felt the cool air rising from the
rushing water and a return of strength in the river's promise
of relief.*

*A gendarme dismounted from his horse, the soles of his boots
landing only inches from Tarvez' feet. He was gaunt and un-
shaven, and his dark eyes stared down at her without emotion.
Nearby another woman screamed.*

*Tarvez instinctively pressed her daughter to her bare chest,
but the gendarme ripped the baby out of her weak arms and
pushed her to the ground.*

"Vartouhi," she screamed. Tarvez clawed at the back of the gendarme's legs. She lunged at the Turk, grabbing a handful of his uniform. "Vartouhi. Vartouhi."

The gendarme spun around and caught her in the middle of the forehead with his fist. Tarvez fell backward on the sharp rocks. She lifted herself in time to see the gendarme throw her daughter into the water.

"Vartouhi!" Tarvez cried out. She ran to the edge of the river that was suddenly filled with children taken from their mothers. Vartouhi's head floated above the surface, her arms outstretched like the wings of an angel, circling slowly in the rapid current.

Tarvez ran along the riverbank crying. "My baby. My angel." She extended her arms in an angel-like manner as she ran after the child. But soon Vartouhi was gone. All the children were gone. Tarvez dropped to her knees and stared at the spot where she had last seen her daughter. Over the roar of the ravenous current, she could hear the wail of mothers crying for their lost babies. And then the sound of the gendarmes riding off on their horses, leaving the women in the desert to die.

Chapter Two

By the time Arak arrived at Oakwood Park, the heat had driven most of the crowd into the shaded area near the river. The picnickers arranged themselves by family around blankets and redwood tables, drinking from bottles of beer and Coca-Cola and trying to stay cool. The collection of old men, who made a habit of arriving early and grabbing the tables closest to the musicians, eyed the new arrivals.

"Saropian." One of the elders, a thin man who supported himself with a cane even when sitting, called out to Arak. "Two more weeks of this hot sun. You can bet on it. No chance for one of those early September rainstorms."

"Music to my ears, Mr. Badalian." Arak shook the frail man's hand. "I got half my grapes on the ground and the other half still to pick."

"The morning clouds." Badalian squinted through thick glasses. "That's how you tell. They still have the color of summer. Two more weeks. You can bet on it."

"I thank you for the good news." Arak patted the old man on the shoulder and made eye contact with each of the other men at the table before excusing himself.

"My best to your uncle," Badalian said.

Arak scanned the crowd as he moved. It was his favorite time of the week. Every Sunday from late spring until the end of the fall harvests, Armenians throughout the valley gathered along the banks of the Kings River. The faces were familiar, even when the names were not. New arrivals and visiting relatives were embraced, their membership in the community assured by a common heritage.

Arak spied his Uncle Henry sitting at one of the shaded tables, holding a beer by the neck and sharing a laugh with a young couple

Arak recognized as new residents in the valley. It was a common scene at any Armenian gathering. Henry was one of a handful of men everyone in the community admired. People listened when he spoke, deferred to his judgment in discussions, and sought him out for advice. It was stature earned in part through financial success, but also, Arak had come to understand, by the way Henry carried himself. Arak had occasional dreams of being as wealthy as Henry, but his real desire was to someday inherit the position of respect his uncle enjoyed.

The young man and his wife both shook Henry's hand before departing, leaving Henry alone at the table with his best friend, Babeg Bedrosian. Babeg was half the size of Henry, with wavy silver hair and comically large ears. His eyes seemed to bulge from his face, which gave an appearance of urgency to everything he said.

"We were talking about that son-of-a-bitch Charlie Chaplin," Babeg said as Arak approached. "He thinks communism is so good, let him live in Russia for a while. Try living in what's become of Armenia these days. One week. Just one week, and he'd see how good we got it."

"I wasn't sure you'd make it today," Henry said.

"Hard to get away during picking season, that's the truth," Babeg said.

"You'd know that better than anyone," Arak said.

Babeg had managed Henry's farming operations for more than 20 years. When a pair of mild heart attacks forced his retirement the previous summer, no one was surprised that Arak took his place. Other men had worked at Saropian Farms longer. But only Arak was family.

"I got to talk to you," Arak said to Henry. "About business."

"On a Sunday?" Henry motioned toward the tables of people that surrounded them. "Can't it wait?"

"I wouldn't bring it up if I didn't have to."

Henry set his bottle on the table. Babeg did the same.

"I heard a couple of hours ago," Arak said. "Hirasuna's paying four cents a tray."

"Are you sure?" Henry said. "Since when?"

"Starting today. Kevorkian told me, and he talked to Hirasuna himself."

"And the contractor agreed?"

"What choice does he have? There's more pickers this year than ever."

"Those Japs," Babeg said. "Always figuring the edge. We could learn a lot from them about how to run a business."

"Anyone besides Hirasuna?" Henry asked.

"It's only a matter of time," Arak said.

Henry took a sip of beer while considering the information. "Most of them are hard workers. They give us a good day's work."

"We all work hard," Arak said.

"They have families to support."

"Everyone's going to be paying four cents by tomorrow," Arak said.

"Then we'll have to do the same," Henry said. "Four cents. Starting tomorrow."

"I'll tell them in the morning."

"We can't pay four and a half if no one else is."

"We can't."

"Explain to them that we have no choice."

"I'll take care of it."

***

The expanse of people spilling into the park was even larger than Teresa had imagined. Most of the women wore brightly colored blouses and skirts. Fierce reds and dark blues, even in the summer heat. Children stirred noisily underfoot, while the men moved about with apparent purpose. Everywhere black and deep brown hair highlighted olive complexions and complemented intensely dark eyes. Each person fit perfectly into the scene before her like pieces in a mosaic. As she watched the gathering from the parking lot, she became keenly aware of an urge to turn around and run.

"I must be crazy about you to put myself through this," she said.

"You did just fine at the cemetery," Mihran said. "Unfortunately, fiancés come with families."

"Not all of them." At that moment, the concept of family seemed more foreign to her than ever. "And how many fiancés also come with an entire ethnic community?"

Mihran pulled blankets and an apricot pie from the trunk of her car. "Ready for round two?"

"You make it sound like a fight," Teresa said. "Is this going to be a battle between me and the Saropians?"

"Let's start over." He placed the pie back in the trunk, paused a second, then lifted it again. "Ready for the second act?"

"Better."

"Like it or not, you're on stage today."

"We're on stage today."

"I might be on the bill," Mihran said. "But you're the main attraction."

"We'll sit with your family, right?"

"As if we had any other choice."

"And your mother will be here?"

"Of course."

That was the good news. From the moment she had heard the story that morning, Teresa could not stop thinking about her future mother-in-law. Tarvez had lost everything. Husband, child, home. Almost her life. How does anyone recover from that? Yet here she was, decades later, her survival nothing short of a miracle, surrounded by a second family and friends. And where was the bitterness? The mistrust? She had taken Teresa's hand a few weeks earlier after Mihran had stumbled through introductions. Had pressed the hand to her chest, as if to say that life was too short to take anything but the most direct route. *Bari galust*, she had said. And although Teresa had never heard the words before, no translation was necessary. Welcome.

"And what did we decide about religion?" Mihran asked.

"Catholic," Teresa said. "Tell them I'm Catholic."

"And which church did you attend this morning?" Mihran said. "In case they ask. Which they probably will."

"The Catholic church near the college. The one where the students go."

"And does this Catholic church have a name?"

"I don't know," Teresa said. "Pick a saint. They're all the same."

As they approached the rows of tables, a small man beckoned them with waving arms and a raspy voice.

"Young lovers! Young lovers!"

"Who's that?" Teresa said under her breath.

"Uncle Babeg," Mihran said. "Babeg Bedrosian."

"Mother's side or father's side?"

"No relation."

The smiling man pressed Teresa's hand between his own. "So this is your girl, Mihran?"

"She's the one." Mihran made the introductions.

"I hope you are not the jealous type, Mihran," Babeg said. "I might just ask your pretty girlfriend here to dance. And I'm warning you. Even at my age, I can be a rascal."

"Consider me warned," Mihran said. "Now, if you'll excuse us, Uncle Babeg. I have to show this lovely thing off to a lot more people."

"A pleasure." Babeg looked Teresa directly in the eye. "I got to tell you. That Mihran is one lucky guy."

Teresa waited until they were several steps away before speaking. "Christ, are they all going to be like that?"

"You enchanted him, you lovely thing you."

"And are you going to talk like that all afternoon?"

"It's what they expect."

Mihran made a point of setting the pie in the middle of the Saropian table and announcing that Teresa had done the baking. Within minutes they were surrounded by a stream of picnickers. In rapid succession, Mihran introduced Teresa to neighbors and friends. Her arrival had been widely anticipated.

She made it through the first wave with prepared phrases and a lot of smiles. When the crowd cleared, Teresa found herself standing across the table from a slightly overweight woman close to her own age. Had to be Serena, Teresa reasoned. Arak's wife and her future sister-in-law. Which would make the two girls sitting on the nearby blanket in matching yellow dresses their daughters. Ages 2 and 4, Teresa remembered, but for the moment the names escaped her.

"I been looking forward to meeting you." Serena flashed a broad smile and introduced herself. "You go to college, don't you?"

"That's right."

"That would make you and Mihran the only ones in the family."

Mihran wrapped his arm around Teresa's shoulder. "Let's not rush this 'family' talk just yet. You might scare her away."

"I thought about going to college." Serena glanced at her daughters. "I still might someday. Wouldn't that be something? Two

Saropian women with college educations?" Serena caught herself. "I mean, if you two decide to get married."

"Definitely would make us the talk of Armenian Town," Mihran said.

"Can I help with something?" Teresa asked.

Serena handed her bowls of rice and wheat pilaf to set on the table, followed by plates of eggplant, zucchini and tomatoes.

"I made these with *Mayr* in her kitchen last night." Serena held out a platter of *yalanchi* for Teresa's inspection. "You ever stuff grape leaves before?"

"No, but I'm looking forward to learning," Teresa said.

"We'll make an Armenian out of her yet," Mihran said.

"What sort of foods did your mother teach you?" Serena asked Teresa. "I mean, your last name's Twomey, right? What kind of nationality is that?"

"I'm half Irish," Teresa said. "We're Irish as far back on my father's side as anyone can trace."

"Arak would say that makes you all Irish," Serena said. "You got an Irish last name, you're Irish. It doesn't matter what the other half is. Somehow when you get married, you become whatever your husband's name says you are. Of course, I was already Armenian before I married Arak."

"My mother's side is pretty mixed," Teresa said. "Her father was Dutch-German, and her mother was from Guadalajara."

"Where's that?"

"Mexico."

Serena paused. The plate of baklava she held in her hand hovered above the table. "You're part Mexican?"

"One quarter."

"Wait until Arak hears about this." Serena turned to Mihran. "You didn't tell us your girlfriend was part Mexican."

"I've been working my way down the list," Mihran said. "Teresa's heritage comes right after where she buys her clothes and just before her favorite flavor of ice cream. I was planning to get there sometime next week."

"There was a girl who used to live over on Fulton that was half Mexican," Serena said. "Jenny Minasian. She didn't look Mexican either. But her kids sure did."

One of the girls began to cry. Serena eyed her daughter for a moment, but before she could decide on a response, an elderly woman stepped out from a nearby crowd and tended to the girl.

"Grandma's got it," Serena declared.

Teresa did her best to stay in the conversation, but her attention was drawn to the woman and the granddaughter. Tarvez carefully lifted the child. Without speaking, she placed an open palm against the girl's teary cheek. The child searched her grandmother's face for a few seconds and stopped crying. Tarvez pressed the girl to her chest and, after a minute, placed her back on the blanket next to her sister.

Henry, Babeg and Arak arrived with plates of marinated lamb, peppers and onions hot off the grill. Serena instructed everyone to take a seat before the food got cold. She insisted that Teresa sit next to her.

"So much to eat," Teresa said.

"That's the way we Armenians do it," Serena said.

Serena barraged her with questions throughout the meal, while Babeg, who sat directly across from her, took it upon himself to educate her about Armenian culture and history. All of which was fine with Teresa. She could handle these two. Survival was the primary goal for the day.

Dessert was presented with a flourish. The women loaded everyone's plate with baklava, fresh berries and a slice from Teresa's apricot pie. Before Teresa could take her first bite, the music started. Heads turned at nearby tables, and people rose.

"Mihran," Babeg said. "You going to dance with this girl or am I?"

Mihran extended an upturned palm to Teresa. "Shall we?"

It took her a moment to realize that he was not joking. Dozens of couples were making their way toward the music.

"I'm afraid I don't know how," Teresa said.

"You don't have to know anything," Serena said. "Mihran can teach you."

"She's right," Mihran said. "Inexperience is no excuse."

Teresa saw no option but surrender. She took Mihran's hand.

"I thought you could use a break," Mihran said when they were out of earshot.

"How did I do?"

"They all love you," Mihran said. "And the pie was a nice touch."

"Shows I have the domestic skills of a real wife?"

"Exactly. Just don't use words like *domestic* in front of them."

Groups of dancers—some couples, but also combinations of three, four and sometimes five—filled the grassy area in front of the musicians. The three band members, all in their fifties or older, already sported beads of perspiration on their foreheads. Every instrument they played was foreign to Teresa. There was something that looked like a dulcimer, a two-sided, hand-held drum, and some kind of flute or oboe painted pink and gold. The dancers moved in lines with their arms around each other's waists. Some of the men waved red, orange or blue handkerchiefs as they pivoted on their heels, right and then left, occasionally hopping or stamping their feet.

"The *tamzara*," Mihran said. "Very traditional dance."

"You really think someone with red hair belongs out there?" Teresa said.

"Just watch for a minute. It's not as difficult as it looks."

To Teresa's relief, the dancers were far from synchronized. Lines broke apart and came back together as steps were added and omitted. No matter how badly they stumbled, everyone kept dancing. But the pattern escaped her. She was about to tell Mihran that she found the dance impossible when the music stopped. Dancers and spectators clapped and cheered. The drummer beat his instrument in reply.

"Darn," Teresa said. "Just when I was beginning to get the hang of it."

Another song started up.

"Bar dance." Mihran grabbed Teresa by the wrist. "Even a redhead can do this."

He pulled her into the middle of the dancers, who seemed to be moving at random around them. Mihran locked his little finger onto hers and lifted their hands. A plump woman in a wide orange hat locked onto Teresa's other little finger, and she suddenly found herself part of a large, moving circle.

Mihran shouted instructions. "Right. Left over right. Point with your left, now with the right."

Teresa focused on the basic step. Right, then left over right. The pattern repeated itself after only a few bars. One of the musicians let out a piercing squeal. Teresa ducked to avoid a waving handkerchief. She moved left when everyone else moved right but quickly recovered. The woman's orange hat flew off. A gray-haired man in a billowing yellow and red shirt took her place. He sang as he danced. Teresa stopped looking at her feet. She started to anticipate the next step. Soon she was moving in rhythm with men and women she did not know within a line of dancers amid dozens of other lines of dancers. Everyone swaying and stepping and stumbling and laughing together. And for the first time, Teresa wondered if maybe, just maybe, she could be a part of this.

Chapter Three

The end of the Sunday event was always determined by the band. When the music stopped, the picnickers began the slow process of ending conversations, persuading someone to eat the last of the food, promising to visit, and gathering up the blankets and dishes and kids.

Arak sat across the table from Babeg, half listening to his predecessor talk about the advantages of Thompson Seedless over other raisin grapes. He had positioned himself so that he could easily catch the eye of anyone passing by. As he surveyed the diminishing crowd, Arak noticed three young men rapidly approaching. Their pace and the way they flailed their arms as they spoke suggested a level of agitation that was out-of-place at the picnic.

"Arak. Arak," one of the men called out. Arak recognized him as Kemar, a small and excitable young man who sometimes did seasonal work on the farm. "We got trouble."

"What kind of trouble?" Arak asked.

"Turks."

Kemar pointed toward the barbeque pits, but all Arak could see were the cooks scraping the grills and nearby picnickers collected their things.

"What are you talking about?"

"Five of them," Kemar said. "Three men and two women. Got here about an hour ago. And they're all Turks."

"How do you know?"

"No one's ever seen them before." Kemar's voice was getting louder as he spoke. "Someone asked them where they're from. They said Fresno. Then one of them says Istanbul. That's Turkey, isn't it?"

"That's crazy talk," Babeg said. "Why would Turks come to an Armenian picnic?"

"Why would they say they're from Turkey if they're not?" Kemar said.

"I've never seen a Turk in Fresno," Babeg said. "Where would they live? There's no Turks in this entire valley."

The conversation was starting to draw attention. Men from nearby tables approached to see what was going on, while the women watched from a distance. Mihran stopped playing with his nieces and joined the group.

"Someone said they're students," Kemar said. "Said they live by the college."

"Why would someone from Turkey come all the way here just to go to college?" Babeg said. "There's colleges everywhere. Even in Turkey."

"All kinds of people go to college here." Kemar pointed to Mihran. "Don't they?"

"That's true," Mihran said. "I've seen some Chinese and some Japanese. Even a few from India."

"But from Turkey?" Babeg asked.

Mihran shrugged. "It's a big school."

A volley of opinions spewed from the crowd. *We don't want no Turks here. Sons of murderers. Maybe they're from down south. Maybe LA. No one invited them.*

Arak raised his arm. Much to his satisfaction, the outpouring of voices instantly ceased. All eyes were on him.

"The first thing we do is find out who these people are." Arak started toward the barbeque area. Several men, including Mihran and Babeg, followed.

"Them." Kemar pointed to two men and two women making their way across the park toward the parking lot. "Those people over there."

Arak positioned himself directly in the strangers' path. The men formed a semi-circle around him.

"Excuse me." Arak stood with his feet apart and his hands at his side. "I don't think I've seen you at one of these picnics before."

The smaller of the two men stepped forward and smiled. He was several years younger than Arak, with smooth features and high rounded eyebrows. His poor attempt at growing a moustache only highlighted how young he was.

"We are here for the first time." The man spoke with an accent, but not one Arak recognized. "We heard about the shish kabob and the music. We came to enjoy ourselves."

"Are you Armenian?" Arak asked.

"We are Turkish." The man made the point without hesitation and even with a hint of pride. "The food and the music are very much like what we know from our home."

The Turk's companions nodded in agreement. They smiled at Arak as if thanking him.

"What makes you think you're welcome here?" Arak said.

"We heard all were invited," the Turk said.

"All Armenians," Kemar said.

Arak held up an open palm to indicate that he would handle the matter.

"I think it's time for you and your friends to go," Arak said.

Another smile crossed his face as the Turk seemed to consider the possibility that Arak was joking. "We have much in common. There were many Armenians in Turkey at one time, yes? And then they left."

Arak could sense the tightening of muscles among the men who surrounded him. A few shifted their weight. Someone coughed.

"Armenians didn't leave Turkey," Arak said. "They were forced out."

"Forced out?" The man looked to his companions as if seeking an explanation.

"Forced out and murdered," Kemar yelled. "By Turks."

Traces of fear came and went from the Turk's expression. He glanced among the crowd as if looking for a friendly face. But before he could reply, another man joined the group and pushed the young man aside.

"Who are you?" The newcomer stared at Arak with impatient eyes. His features were hard and square, and he wore a neatly trimmed beard. "What is going on?"

"I was telling your friends here to leave," Arak said.

"And why is that? What have they done?"

"It's not what you've done. It's who you are."

"You don't know us."

"I know you're Turks. I know what your people did to my people."

"You want us to leave, fine." The man hoisted a cloth bag over his shoulder to indicate that the conversation was over. "But keep your lies about the Turkish people to yourself."

The five Turks started to walk around the gathering of Armenian men, but Arak moved quickly to cut them off. The bearded man set his bag to the side and faced Arak.

Everyone fell silent. The two men stood eye to eye. It was the kind of moment Arak lived for. A chance to demonstrate to everyone who he was and what he stood for.

"Armenians didn't leave Turkey," Arak said. "They were murdered."

The Turk gave no indication of backing down. "If Armenians died, it is because they were traitors. Breaking laws and giving aid to the Russians. The Turkish government had to defend itself."

Arak pointed a finger at the bearded man's chest. The Turk did not flinch.

"You and your friends are leaving now." Arak accented his words by jabbing the tip of his finger within inches of the other man's shirt. "You're leaving, and you're not coming back."

"It seems we are outnumbered here," the Turk replied in a voice that yielded nothing. "So, as you please. We will leave now."

This time Arak let them go. The three men and two women moved at an unhurried pace across the length of the park. The collection of men standing behind Arak watched the procession in silence. Not one Turk glanced back.

"And never return!" Kemar yelled when the Turks reached the parking lot. A few others echoed the remark and tossed out their own insults. Arak chose not to stop them.

Then suddenly Arak found himself surrounded. The men shook his hand and patted his back. He led them back to the remaining picnickers who had watched the encounter from a distance.

The story spread quickly. Arak stood up to the Turks. He told them to leave and not come back. Witnesses recreated the scene for those who had not been there, who in turn retold the story to others. Arak made his way to the Saropian table and tried to busy himself by folding tablecloths and blankets. But he was fully aware of the attention he was drawing. Several times he heard his name rising from a nearby conversation. He quietly absorbed the admiration. The men had come to him. Not to one of the elders. Not to his Uncle

Henry. Out of all the people at the picnic, they had come to him. And he had not let them down.

Chapter Four

Mihran loaded the last of the blankets and leftovers into Teresa's car. A few more good-byes, and they would be on their way. He found Teresa where he had left her, with Serena and her two daughters. Teresa caught and held his gaze in a way that said she was more than ready to leave.

Mihran stepped to Teresa's side to signal that they were set to go, but it took several more minutes for Serena to wind down the conversation. After Teresa accepted an awkward hug and it looked like they were finally leaving, Arak approached.

"I need to talk with Mihran about something," Arak said.

"Can't it wait?" Serena said. "We got to get these girls home."

"You and the girls can go with your new friend." Arak motioned toward Teresa. "Mihran can ride home with me."

Serena looked to Mihran, who shrugged his shoulders. She apologized to Teresa, who believably insisted that the arrangement was not a problem, then helped Ana and Eliz into the back seat of Teresa's car.

"Call me?" Teresa said to Mihran.

"Of course."

"I need to know how I did."

"I can tell you right now. Terrific."

"I'm going to need a lot more reassurance than that."

They kissed good-bye. Mihran made his way to Arak's red and white Ford coupe and was not surprised to find the car was empty. He spied his brother standing in a circle with four other men several cars away. Even at that distance Mihran could see the men basking in his brother's moment and Arak's delight in allowing them to do so.

It was another 30 minutes before they got on the road. The oak trees that ran along the banks of the river cast long shadows across the pavement, and a few of the approaching cars had already turned on their headlights.

"Henry wanted me to ask you something," Arak said. "He's thinking about buying Karabian's old farm."

"The place out near Sanger?" Mihran asked. "That's all cotton, isn't it?"

"Henry likes the idea of expanding into cotton. But it will make managing the farm more difficult."

"Let me guess. He's looking to hire someone."

"Just to look after the cotton business," Arak said. "Mostly bookkeeping stuff. That person would work under me, of course."

"I thought we settled this."

"Henry wanted me to ask."

"Nothing's changed," Mihran said. "I have other plans. I'm going to college."

"That's what I told him you would say."

They both tolerated a moment of silence.

"You know it's nothing personal," Mihran said. "I just want to do something else with my life."

"I'd say Henry's done pretty well for himself," Arak said. "And without a college degree."

"It's not about money."

"Right. Who the hell wants to work on a farm?"

"That's not what I meant."

They turned onto Highway 99. Although it was the main artery connecting a string of farming towns up and down the valley, the road bore little traffic this late on a Sunday evening.

"It wouldn't really be farm work," Arak said. "It's not like you'd have to get your hands dirty."

"I don't see any reason to keep talking about this."

"Fine with me." Arak grabbed at his shirt pocket. "I need cigarettes."

Vincent's Grocery sat 50 feet off the highway, separated from the road by a large, unpaved parking lot. The windows across the front of the store were covered with so many signs promoting beer and cigarettes that Mihran could not tell at first whether the lights were on. They pulled up next to the only other car in the lot, a black

Mercury badly in need of washing. Arak started up the wood-planked steps that ran across the front of the building with Mihran trailing behind.

Just as they reached the top step, the screen door squeaked open, and the brothers found themselves face-to-face with the bearded Turk and one of the women from the picnic. Everyone froze.

"I think you ought to keep moving," Arak said.

The Turk's eyes narrowed. He held a bag of groceries in one arm. The woman released a barely audible "Oh" as the door slammed shut behind them.

"Of course, we are leaving." The Turk cupped the woman's shoulder with his free arm and directed her toward the parking lot. "We have the right to come and go as we please."

Arak watched the man set the groceries in the car. The Turk did not look back until he reached the driver-side door.

"You talk tough when you have a gang around you," he yelled. "Or when you are talking to a man standing next to his wife. You better hope I never find you alone. If you Armenians had any fight in you at all, you would not be a displaced people."

Mihran grabbed his brother's sleeve. "Let it go, Arak."

Arak jerked his arm free and started down the steps.

"It's not worth it, Arak."

The Mercury quickly backed away. The Turk put the car into drive and headed out of the lot. Arak stood at the bottom of the steps and watched them go.

But before reaching the road, the driver turned the car so that his side faced the brothers. He rolled down the window.

"Cowards," he yelled.

Arak charged toward the Mercury. He reached the car in time to pound his fist against the rear fender, the heavy dull thud punctuating the whine of the engine. Squealing tires sent a cloud of loose dirt into the air. Pieces of gravel pinged the underside of the car as the Turk and his wife sped off.

Arak stood in the powdery dust rubbing the side of his hand and watching the round taillights disappear down the highway.

"Bastards." Arak joined his brother at the top of the steps. "I hope I at least put a dent in his fender."

The fragrance of overripe cantaloupe greeted them as they entered the store. Mihran nodded to Vincent behind the counter. A small electric fan whirred on a shelf above the cash register with no noticeable effect.

Arak pulled a pack of Pall Malls from a display and dropped a dollar on the worn linoleum counter.

Vincent recorded the purchase in a small receipt book.

"I guess you do business with anyone who's got the right color money," Arak said.

Vincent rang open the cash register without comment.

"Those people who were just in here. Did you know they're Turks?"

The store owner shrugged to indicate that the information meant nothing to him.

"We don't care much for Turks," Arak said. "I chased them out of our picnic this afternoon."

"Don't matter to me." Vincent handed Arak his change. "You had it right what you said about the color of their money."

Arak lit a cigarette before they reached the car. "Damned Italian doesn't care about anything but making money. I'd like to see that Turkish bastard try to buy something in Armenian Town."

Mihran responded with a noncommittal hum, which he hoped would show support without encouragement.

They drove in silence. As soon as Arak turned off the highway and onto Clovis Avenue, Mihran noticed the distinctive small taillights on the vehicle in front of them. Although at least a quarter of a mile away, there was no doubt about the type of car.

"Look who's here," Arak said.

"It's not the same Mercury," Mihran said. "They'd be farther away by now."

"Maybe they stopped for something." Arak pressed the accelerator. "Maybe they needed gas."

"What are you doing, Arak?"

"Let's just see if these are our friends."

Arak pulled to within a few feet of the Mercury's bumper. It was difficult to make out the figures in the dim evening light, but when the headlights from an oncoming car outlined the heads and shoulders of the driver and his passenger, there was no doubt.

"Let's have some fun." Arak inched the Ford closer.

"Don't be stupid, Arak."

"I'm just going to scare them a little."

"This is not funny."

"It's not meant to be."

Arak flashed his lights twice but got no reaction. He tapped once on the horn. The Turk sped up.

"Now we're getting somewhere." Arak closed the gap between the vehicles. The Mercury accelerated.

"Don't be a fool," Mihran said.

"Don't tell me what to do."

Arak pulled to within inches of the Mercury's bumper and leaned on the horn. Mihran glanced at the speedometer. 50 mph. Again the Turk sped up. Arak matched his speed. Rows of peach trees and fields of cotton whisked past on either side.

"We're going to reach the city pretty soon," Mihran said. "There's a stop sign coming up."

"Not for a couple of miles."

Arak pulled alongside the Mercury as if he were going to pass on the two-lane road. The nose of his car inched slightly ahead of the Turk's. He tugged quickly on the steering wheel and then back, swerving enough to give the impression that he was cutting the Mercury off. The Turk responded by pulling so far to the edge of the road that his right tires left the asphalt. The car traveled for several yards on the shoulder before returning to the road and speeding up.

Arak dropped back behind the Turk and howled. "He thinks he can outrun me with that piece of shit."

"That's enough, Arak," Mihran said. "You're going to get somebody killed."

"Somebody ought to kill those sonsabitches."

Arak again pulled slightly ahead of the other car and made the same swerving motion, which again caused the Turk to drive halfway off the side of the road. A car approached from the other direction. Arak dropped back until the road was clear, then quickly returned to the left lane alongside the Mercury.

"Pull over and let me out," Mihran said.

"You say you want me to pull over?" Arak again swerved close enough to give the appearance that he was running the Turk off the road. But the Turk held his ground. Arak's front fender bumped against the Mercury, sending the Turk's car off the pavement. This time, the car found an irrigation trough.

The right front wheel dipped into the trough. The rear of the Mercury skidded sideways, barely missing Arak's bumper. The car flipped on its side, then rolled into a roadside orchard. At the end of a full circle, the Mercury smashed into the side of an almond tree. The crunch of metal filled the air. The tree trunk snapped in two.

Arak pulled to the side of the road, and the brothers leapt from their car. Except for the dust settling around the wreck, all was still. The felled tree was spread across the hood of the Mercury. The windows were shattered, the roof flattened almost to the top of the seats. There were no signs of movement inside the vehicle.

Mihran stood in the diminishing light trying to make sense of the scene before him. The reverberating roar of crunching metal and crashing glass overwhelmed his senses, and for the briefest part of a moment he was seized by a wave of disbelief. A surge of panic left his arms weak and his legs numb. But he forced two large breaths. A rising sense of responsibility demanded that he act.

He started to run toward the orchard, but Arak called out to him.

"Don't be crazy," Arak yelled. "Let's get out of here."

"We have to do something."

"We have to get out of here."

"But they might need help."

"The next car down the road can help," Arak said. "We need to be as far away from here as possible."

"They'll know it was us," Mihran said.

"No one will know it was us. Not if we leave right now." He waved for his brother to get back in the car.

Mihran glanced once more at the still-silent vehicle in the orchard.

"I'm your brother, damn it," Arak said. "For my sake. Get in the car now."

Mihran studied Arak's face. This was as close to pleading as he had ever heard from his brother. He returned to the car and got inside.

Arak checked the rearview mirror repeatedly until they reached the stop sign at Kings Canyon Road. No cars in either direction. Ten minutes later, they were home. Arak turned off the ignition, but neither of them moved.

"This never happened," Arak said. "You understand? This thing tonight with the cars never happened."

Chapter Five

Henry eased himself into the overstuffed chair. Arak and Mihran sat across from him on the couch. Only the clatter of dishes and silverware from the kitchen interrupted the silence.

Serena set three cups with saucers on the coffee table. "Can I bring you anything else?"

"This is fine," Henry said. "Thank you."

"Go to the bedroom and close the door," Arak said to his wife.

"I've got some cleaning up to do in the kitchen," Serena said.

"Leave it."

Henry sipped his coffee and waited for the house to quiet. His nephews knew to wait until he was ready.

"Tell me the whole story," Henry said. "Starting with this afternoon, at the picnic. We have plenty of time. I want all the facts, not just the ones you choose to remember or the ones you want me to hear."

Arak started. He described in detail the confrontation at the park, the meeting at Vincent's, the car chase down Clovis Avenue and the crash. Except for an occasional glance at his brother, he looked directly at his uncle while telling the story. Neither Henry nor Mihran said a word until Arak leaned back on the couch to indicate that he was finished.

"Do you have anything to add?" Henry asked Mihran.

Mihran shook his head.

"Do you think they could have survived the accident?" Henry asked.

"Hard to say," Arak said.

"It was pretty bad," Mihran said. "The car rolled over. The roof caved in."

"If they survive," Henry said, "could they identify you?"

"It was getting dark," Arak said. "And we were driving pretty fast."

"But we pulled alongside them three times," Mihran said. "They had to at least suspect who it was. Especially after seeing us at Vincent's."

"Could you see the driver's face?" Henry asked.

"Impossible," Arak said. "It was too dark."

"But you were on the other side of the car," Henry said. "Mihran, what could you see?"

"Only an outline through the window," Mihran said. "I don't remember the driver ever turning to face us. But he had to know. I mean, who else could it be?"

"Any witnesses?" Henry asked.

"Not that I saw," Arak said.

"But you didn't look for witnesses until after the accident," Henry said. "You drove, what? Three or four miles down Clovis Avenue? How can you be sure no one saw you speeding by?"

Arak looked away.

"Did anyone see you at Vincent's?" Henry asked.

"No one," Arak said.

"Vincent saw you," Henry said.

"He was inside," Arak said. "The door was closed. And you can't see through those windows because of all the signs."

"How many men were with you when you talked to the Turks at the picnic?" Henry asked.

"Who would say anything?" Arak said.

"That wasn't the question," Henry said.

Arak shrugged. "Six or seven, maybe."

"Plus the Turks," Henry said. "And what about your car? It's sitting in front of the house right now, isn't it? Did your car come into contact with the Mercury?"

"Only a little bump," Arak said.

"Enough to leave paint from your car on his?" Henry asked.

"Their car was in pretty bad shape," Arak said. "It rolled over. I doubt if you could find a little scratch of paint."

"And what about paint from the Mercury on your car?"

"I didn't think to look."

Everyone took a long sip of coffee.

"Here's what we do," Henry said. "You remember Ruth Hodoian's boy, Stephen? He moved to Glendale last summer and opened his own business. A body shop. I'll call Stephen. Arak will drive the car to Glendale. Tomorrow, if we can arrange it. The sooner the car is out of town, the better. In the meantime, before you go to bed tonight, put it in the garage."

"There's no room in the garage," Arak said.

"Then you'll make room."

"Of course."

"We can't deny what happened at the picnic," Henry said. "The Turks' friends will certainly tell their side of the story. Expect the police to come looking for you."

"And what do I tell them?" Arak said.

"That you told the Turks to leave the picnic," Henry said. "Then you packed up and drove home without incident."

"So if there's no car with paint on it and no one saw the accident," Arak said. "Then there's no evidence. No proof I had anything to do with it."

"Better than that," Henry said. "We've got Mihran to back up your story."

Henry turned to Mihran and was not surprised to find doubt in his nephew's eyes.

"You will support your brother, won't you, Mihran?"

"What about the people in that car?" Mihran asked.

"What about them?" Arak said.

"You ran them off the road," Mihran said. "Their car was destroyed. They have to be injured pretty badly."

"We know that," Arak said.

"They didn't deserve it, Arak."

"It was an accident."

"They might have been killed."

"The guy should have kept his mouth shut."

"And what about the woman?" Mihran asked. "What did she do?"

"They're Turks," Arak said. "He called me a coward. He said Armenians deserved to be murdered."

"And so he deserves to die?"

"Enough." Henry raised an open palm. "Mihran. If the police ask you what happened, what are you going to tell them?"

Mihran folded his arms across his chest and exhaled loudly.

"What will you tell them?" Henry asked.

"What if they survive the accident?" Mihran asked. "They know it was Arak who ran them off the road. They'll tell the police. And then what?"

"It will be their word against yours," Henry said.

"A lot of people saw what happened at the picnic," Mihran said.

"We won't deny that Arak told the Turks to leave. But they were the ones who showed up where they weren't wanted. Telling them to leave is no crime."

Mihran stared at the far wall. Henry knew he had no choice but to wait.

"The car rolled over," Mihran said. "The roof collapsed."

"We've been over this already," Arak said.

"And what if they die, Arak?" Mihran said. "What if you killed two people? What would you say then?"

"I'd say two dead Turks hardly evens the score."

"Stop!" This time Henry rose from his chair. "This is no longer about the two people in that car. Nothing we do or say will change what happened. We are now talking about family. Your family, Mihran."

Henry waited a moment for the words to sink in before settling back in his chair.

"Mihran, you have a choice to make," Henry said. "A choice between your family and the two people in that car. It's as simple as that. When the police ask you what happened, what are you going to say?"

"It's not that simple," Mihran said. "Arak did a terrible thing."

"He did indeed," Henry said. "But you still need to choose."

"What if they die?"

"I hope they do not. But that won't change what you need to do."

"This never should have happened."

"But it did," Henry said. "And now you need to decide. What are you going to tell the police?"

Mihran closed his eyes. Henry and Arak endured an intensely quiet moment.

"Arak and I stopped at Vincent's." Mihran kept his eyes closed while he spoke. "Then we drove straight home. Without incident."

Chapter Six

The first thing Teresa noticed were the white tea roses planted along the side of porch. Just like the ones Tarvez had taken to the cemetery the previous morning. She paused on the sidewalk in front of the well-kept yard and asked herself again what she hoped to accomplish. What she knew for certain was that she was drawn to Mihran's mother. The self-assurance. The tenderness. The graceful generosity. What did the woman know? What elusive insight did Tarvez possess that granted such peace of mind? If anyone understood survival, it was her future mother-in-law.

"Good morning, dear." Tarvez smiled broadly as she opened the door. "What a pleasant surprise."

"I wanted to return your dishware." Teresa lifted the two ceramic plates she carried to emphasize the point. "I had the yalanchi *and* the lamb for dinner last night. I couldn't resist."

"Please come inside."

Teresa stepped into the living room then struggled to hide her disappointment when she saw through the open doorway two women sitting at the kitchen table. She thought she remembered the plump woman in the lime green blouse from the picnic. She was less sure about the other one, whose wavy dark hair spilled out from under an orange and red scarf. Both appeared to be about Tarvez' age. A plate of pastry sat between them.

"Why don't you stay and have coffee?" Tarvez said.

"I see you have guests," Teresa said.

"Guests?" The round woman let out a hearty laugh that seemed to fill the small kitchen. "Is that what we are, Juliana? Guests?"

"Isabel and Juliana," Tarvez said. "My neighbors. We girls sometimes get together for coffee in the morning. Please, join us."

"We could use some new gossip," Juliana called out. "We run out of people to talk about after a while." The two women fell into a bout of laughter.

Teresa considered how to excuse herself and leave. This arrangement was not at all what she had imagined, and the joyful mood was completely at odds with the state of mind that had brought her here. But before she could say anything, Tarvez placed a gentle hand on her shoulder and again asked her to stay.

"I'd love to," Teresa said.

She joined the two women at the table. Tarvez placed a tiny porcelain cup and matching saucer in front of her. The intricate blue, red and gold pattern seemed out-of-place next to the inexpensive spoons and the gray plastic plate that held the pastry. Tarvez moved to the stove where a wide-rimmed copper pot rested on one of the burners. She lifted the pot by its long wooden handle and poured a small amount of thick dark liquid into each woman's cup.

"You ever have Turkish coffee?" Juliana asked. "It's not like the kind they serve you in the restaurants."

"I can't say that I have," Teresa said.

"Why do we call it that?" Isabel said. "How come we name something this good *Turkish* coffee? What's the Turks got to do with it?"

"Maybe that's where it comes from," Juliana said. "Not everything from Turkey has to be bad."

"They still ought to change the name," Isabel said.

"Just sip it," Juliana instructed Teresa. "A little at a time."

Teresa took a taste. A bitter sensation spread across her tongue, followed by a hint of sweetness. The taste lingered long after she swallowed.

"Good, huh?" Juliana said.

"Very good," Teresa said.

"But strong," Isabel said. "Right?"

"Very strong."

The women smiled their approval.

Serena burst through the front door without knocking, a daughter clasped in each hand. She left the girls with a handful of toys on the living room floor and joined the women in the kitchen. She lit up when she saw Teresa.

"Hey, Teresa." Serena got her own cup and saucer from the cupboard. She took the last seat at the table and waited for Tarvez to pour her some coffee. "You really are becoming one of us."

"Try one of these." Isabel pushed the pastry toward Teresa. "*Bourma.* You like walnuts? I put in lots of walnuts."

As if responding to a signal, each of the women helped themselves to the *bourma.* Teresa waited for the others before taking a bite. The taste of cinnamon and sugar went perfectly with the warm and slightly cluttered kitchen.

"I'm the one who shouldn't be eating." Serena tugged at the edges of her blouse, pulling material away from her waistline in a failed effort to hide her weight. "You may not believe this, Teresa. But a few years ago, I was as thin as you."

"You were such a skinny thing back then," Juliana said. "Wasn't she the skinniest thing?"

"Weren't we all once?" Isabel said.

"Of course, that was before the girls." Serena turned to Teresa. "You and Mihran plan to have a lot of kids?"

"Serena don't waste time getting to the good questions," Isabel said. "I was hoping to ask that one myself."

"I thought we would wait until we talked about marriage first," Teresa said.

"Good answer," Juliana said. She and Isabel fell into another spate of laughter.

"You know, Teresa, you're going to shake things up around here," Isabel said. "Most of these men. They want to keep the women at home. Don't get them too educated."

"What are you going to do with this college education?" Juliana asked. "You going to be a teacher? The smart ones always want to be teachers."

"I don't know yet," Teresa said.

"You don't know?" Serena asked.

"Probably not teaching, though."

"You're just getting a college education because you want to?" Isabel asked.

"Something like that."

They let the moment pass by sipping coffee or taking another bite of *bourma.* To Teresa's relief, the conversation shifted to people they knew and the tasks that filled their daily lives. They laughed at stories they obviously had heard before, with one woman occasionally filling in the punch line to another one's anecdote. The joy, Teresa observed, came more from the shared experience than from the tale. And she had to admit, it was more than a little contagious.

She finished the last of her coffee and set the empty cup on her saucer.

"Come on, Teresa," Isabel said. "How you going to know your fortune?"

"I don't follow you," Teresa said.

"Like this." Isabel lifted her now-empty cup to eye level, then placed it upside-side down on her saucer. "We all do it."

"Juliana's the best." Serena took her last sip and set the cup upside down on her saucer. "She looks at the drippings, and the pattern tells her what's in your future."

"Who can explain it?" Juliana said. "It just comes to you."

On another day, with different people, Teresa would have expressed her skepticism. But for the moment, she preferred to be one of the women gathered in the sanctuary of the kitchen sharing stories over morning coffee. She knew it was part play-acting. Like a girl dressing up in her mother's old clothes. But there was something about the way the women talked with one another – an honesty bordering on innocence – that intrigued her. She also knew that she wanted the moment to continue. She turned her cup upside down and placed it on the saucer.

"Give it a minute to take shape," Isabel said. "Then we'll all see."

"It's scary how accurate she can be," Serena said.

Juliana picked up Isabel's cup and stared intently at the insides. "You're going to have a visit from someone you haven't seen in a long time."

"You said that last week." Isabel grabbed another *bourma*. "How come you never see romance in my future?"

"Because I've seen your husband," Juliana said.

More cackling and giggles. Teresa joined in the laughter.

"Now me." Serena handed Juliana her cup. "See if you can tell me what Arak is up to."

"What makes you think your husband is up to anything?" Isabel asked.

"Arak and Henry were talking until late last night," Serena said. "Then today Arak tells me he might have to make a trip, but he won't tell me where or when."

"Probably business," Isabel said. "If it was anything interesting, he wouldn't have told you that much."

"But Mihran was there, too," Serena said. "If it's farm business, why's Mihran involved?"

All eyes turned to Teresa.

"I haven't talked with Mihran since the picnic," Teresa said.

"Sorry, girls," Juliana said, staring into Serena's cup. "It's a business trip."

"I thought it was Serena's fortune in the coffee drippings," Isabel said. "Not her husband's."

Juliana set the cup back on Serena's saucer. "A wife's fortune is tied to her spouse's. For better or worse, right?"

"Do Teresa next," Isabel said. "See if you can find some grandchildren for Tarvez in that cup."

Juliana stared deeply into the coffee drippings. She turned the cup right and left, furrowing her brow and sighing a couple of times.

"Come on, Juliana," Isabel said. "The kids will be in school before you finish looking at that cup."

"Sometimes a person's future is cloudy," Juliana said. "I think maybe there's forces that want Teresa and Mihran to get together, but maybe also some forces that don't."

No one knew quite how to react to this news.

"I think you and Mihran make a wonderful couple," Tarvez said.

"Sure you do," Serena said.

Isabel waved a dismissive hand in Juliana's direction. "This is all for fun, really."

"Of course," Teresa said.

Juliana returned the cup to the empty saucer in front of Teresa. Tarvez started to collect the dishes. The pastry was eaten, and the conversation exhausted. Teresa's morning as one of the neighborhood girls was coming to an end.

Chapter Seven

Arak stared at the phone, the object of his attention all morning. It sat on the corner of the desk, black and silent, drawing out the minutes. The single-room structure that served as his office sat forty feet from the main barn and was the center of activity for Saropian Farms. Pickers reported for work each morning in front of the building and collected their pay each evening at a card table set up next to the office door. When people were told to meet "on the farm," everyone knew this was where they meant.

Arak's muscles ached from too little sleep, yet he remained on edge. Waiting was always harder than acting. Serena hadn't mentioned the late-night meeting with Henry or that the car was now in the garage. Arak told her only that he might be making a sudden trip and that she should pack him a bag. When he didn't elaborate, she knew not to ask.

A ledger with tray counts and payment figures sat open on his desk, but Arak's attention was elsewhere. He went over the details of the plan, rehearsing in his mind the exact phrases he would use when and if he talked to the police. But he also could not stop thinking about the picnic. There were other men they could have gone to. They walked right past Bert Benasian and Ardak Vartikian, both big landowners. Instead, they came to him. And he had done the job. *You and your friends are leaving now. You're leaving, and you're not coming back.* And then there was the accident. He wished things hadn't turned out the way they did, but it was just like his brother to see the situation as more complicated than it was. What Mihran no doubt thought of as sophisticated moral questions struck Arak as nothing more than a lack of basic standards for living your life. Sometimes you have to take sides. And you do what you have to do.

His thoughts were interrupted by a light tapping at the door. He sprang to open it. But instead of Henry or someone sent by his uncle, he found two migrant workers. The visitors stood a respectable distance from the door. They had no expectation that they might be invited inside.

Arak recognized one of them. Roberto had picked grapes for Saropian Farms for as long as Arak could remember. The old man held his hat against the front of his dusty clothes. A dark patch of perspiration lined the collar of his blue shirt. Arak did not know the second man, who stood to the side and slightly behind Roberto. He was small, even for a migrant, but muscular. Early twenties. Years of farm labor would one day leave him with the same stooped shoulders and tired eyes as all the older workers. But for now the young picker stood erect and stared straight ahead. His eyes were hard and clear, and everything about the way he carried himself suggested defiance, like a small man who had to fight all his life to prove his mettle.

"Mister Saropian." Roberto established brief eye contact before dropping his gaze to the floor. "May I speak with you?"

"I haven't got a lot of time today, Roberto. What do you need?"

The worker's fingers twitched where they held the brim of his hat. "The pay, Mr. Saropian. We were told four and a half cents for a tray."

"And that's what you got. Until today."

"But four cents..."

"It's what everybody's paying from now on."

"The difference may not seem like much to you." Roberto lifted his chin briefly to meet Arak's gaze. "But it is a lot of money to the pickers."

"It's a lot of money to the growers, too."

"But four cents..."

"You're a good man, Roberto," Arak said. "And I'd like to help you. But it's out of my hands."

"Yes, sir."

Arak waited for Roberto to excuse himself, but the old worker did not budge.

"There's also the faucets," Roberto said. "The other pickers, they wanted me to say something."

"We're pretty busy this time of year," Arak said.

"The faucets by the living areas. They still don't work."

"We'll get to them when we can."

"We have to walk a long way to get water."

"I'll look into it myself when picking season's over."

Roberto placed his hat back on his head and took a step away from the door while still facing Arak. A sign of respect.

"Another thing," Arak said. "A lot of those trays are coming up light. I'm tired of paying for a full tray when you're only giving me a half."

"I will tell them," Roberto said. "We will give you full trays."

"I'd appreciate it."

Roberto took another step away from the door. But the second man remained.

"Meeting's over," Arak said.

The small man did not move. "I wouldn't call that much of a meeting." Unlike most pickers, this man spoke with almost no accent.

"And just who are you?" Arak asked.

"My name is Enrico. And we came here to talk."

"I heard you talk."

"No. I don't think you did."

"Then I heard all I care to."

"There are other problems with the shacks," Enrico said. "The ones near the road smell like weed killer. Or like something you spray on hornets' nests. The kids who slept there the first night got sick."

"So don't sleep there."

"One boy was bitten by a rat," Enrico said. "Now the family sleeps in their car."

"You want a nice house," Arak said, "you're free to go buy one."

"Roberto told you about these problems last week."

Roberto stared at the ground. The young man was speaking out of turn.

"Let's not forget who works for who," Arak said. "And right now your boss is telling you to get back to work. *Comprende?*"

"I understand." Enrico glanced over Arak's shoulder as if surveying the insides of the office. "We came to you with simple requests. Twice. We won't ask again."

***

It was nearly noon before the call came.

"Everything's arranged," Henry said. "You can be there tonight if you leave right away. Take the car directly to the body shop. You'll spend the night in Glendale, in Stephen's apartment. Come home tomorrow on the Greyhound."

"When will I get my car back?"

"A couple of days. Someone will drive the car here when it's ready."

"Should I take some cash with me?" Arak asked. "How much is this going to cost?"

"It's already taken care of."

"Who do I owe?"

"Don't worry about it," Henry said. "It's taken care of."

Chapter Eight

Mihran had made it through the evening. The chaotic minutes after the accident, the meeting with Henry, the short walk home and the awkward conversation with his mother before going to bed. He had survived by relying on the detachment skills he developed in the army. You simply had to observe the world as if watching scenes in a movie. Everything becomes a series of events happening to someone else. Emotions are genuine but buffered. Like the sadness you experience when watching a newsreel about starving children halfway around the world. The technique had gotten him through Korea. It would get him through this as well.

But the dam had burst sometime before dawn. Mihran woke to the roar of speeding cars, the crunch of broken glass, and the hollow thud of collapsing metal. He sat up in the dark and listened to his heartbeat pulsing through his ears. His damp tee-shirt was pasted onto his skin. There was no use trying to get back to sleep.

He busied himself with his morning routine of showering and dressing and a quick bite before work. But the images were difficult to keep at bay. He experienced them as rapid snippets, like objects seen between boxcars on the other side of a passing train. A young woman, her dress spattered in red. The black Mercury rolling through the orchard. And then, inexplicably, once or twice, there was the grenade thrower. The uniformed man with a featureless face. Then the spray of bullets followed by an intensely cold silence.

***

"You look like hell," Jack said by way of a greeting. It was as close

55

to "good morning" as Mihran had heard in the year and a half he had worked for the man.

"Some kind of bug," Mihran said.

"You're not going to get sick on me," Jack said. "You promised me 40 hours this week. I've been good about letting you work around classes. You know that."

"Not to worry." Mihran took his place behind the cluttered metal desk. "You got me all day."

"Look at this mess." Jack held up a stack of papers. Edges of contracts and legal forms stuck out in odd angles. "Is this any way to run a law office? I ought to get me a real assistant. Someone who knows the business."

"You mean someone you'd have to pay more." The predictable back-and-forth somehow made Mihran feel better.

"Honestly, Mihran. Are you sure you want to be a lawyer?"

"I never said I was going to be a lawyer."

"But you said something like that. You said you wanted to learn about the law."

"I said I wanted to see what it was like to be a lawyer. I said it's something I might consider as a career someday."

"Justice." Jack slapped an open palm against the top of his desk. "That's what you said. You were interested in justice."

"Something like that." Mihran lifted a pile of folders from his in tray.

"I'm not even going to ask what you think now," Jack said. "I tried to tell you I wasn't a trial lawyer. I told you it wasn't like in the movies."

"That's exactly what you told me."

"Twenty-two years," Jack said. "And what have I got to show for it? Just me and a part-time assistant trying to run the whole damned office. Take my advice, Mihran. Think twice about this idea of yours to go to law school."

"I will." Mihran opened the top folder.

"Medical school," Jack said. "That's where the money is."

Work was exactly what Mihran needed. Contracts and deeds. Fill in the blanks. Everything laid out in precise language. Black ink on white paper. Focus on the work, he told himself, and make it through the morning.

***

Eddie's Café always had the radio set on KFRE during the lunch hour. The station's current promotional gimmick was local news every 15 minutes. Mihran sat at the end of the counter and nibbled at some kind of sandwich. He tried to imagine the reporter's account of the accident. *Two people walked away from a one-car accident on Clovis Avenue last night. A few scratches and bruises, but otherwise they were fine.*

It was possible.

He waited until after the 1:00 update before heading back to the office. If there was anything worth reporting about the accident, the radio station did not have it.

At 3:00 Mihran asked Jack if he could take a break. "I need to stretch my legs. Get a little fresh air."

"It's more than a hundred degrees out there," Jack said. "Get your fresh air when you run over to the courthouse."

It was 4:25 before Jack dropped the documents to be taken to the Recorder's Office on Mihran's desk. Mihran bolted out of the office. But instead of heading straight for the courthouse, he stopped at Gideon's Newsstand where he found a stack of *Fresno Bees* piled on the sidewalk. He grabbed a copy of the afternoon paper and slapped a nickel on the counter. Gideon acknowledged the transaction with a sharp nod.

Mihran found what he was looking for in the second section. *Two Hurt in Auto Crash.* But his first attempt to read the article failed. His eyes could only jump from one explosive phrase to the next. *Critical condition. One-car accident. Community Hospital. Police seeking information.*

A man bumped into him. He was standing in the middle of the sidewalk. Mihran folded the paper and headed for the courthouse, but the few words he had been able to process from the article would not let go. *Critical condition.* Critical meant serious. But not fatal. He tried to picture two patients in hospital beds. But he had never been inside a hospital, and the scenes that came to mind were cartoonish images with large, humming machines and nurses in pointy white hats.

He found a shaded bench outside the courthouse where he read the story sentence by sentence. There was no mention of another car, no suggestion that the accident involved anything more than a driver swerving off the road and into the orchard. A one-car accident. Police were investigating. Of course, they were. An investigation would be routine. But if the man and his wife had said something to the police – if they were able to talk—the newspaper reporter did not know about it.

Mihran refolded the newspaper and headed up the courthouse steps, but a bolt of shame brought him to a halt. He reopened the paper. The information he had passed over the first time was in the first paragraph. Emin Aybar and his wife, Hazan. Emin and Hazan. The names were foreign, but not strange. More similar to Armenian than most American names. His mental depictions of the man and the woman were suddenly more detailed. Emin and Hazan Aybar. People with names. With families and friends. Two individuals who happened to cross paths with two other individuals. And now they were in Fresno Community Hospital in critical condition.

Chapter Nine

For the second time that day, Teresa turned her car onto M Street. She eased the vehicle past the Holy Trinity Apostolic Church and into the part of Fresno known as Armenian Town. As often happened when she found herself this close to a church, Teresa's heart began to race. She held a hand to the side of her face to remove the building from view and kept the hand in place until she was more than a block down the street, where she pulled to the side of the road and waited until her muscles relaxed and her breathing returned to normal. Would she ever get over this fear?

Mihran was standing in the front yard reading the newspaper. Teresa slammed the car door a little louder than she needed to but provoked no reaction. Nor was Mihran aware of her opening the gate in the short picket fence and entering the yard.

"Is the light better out here?" she asked.

"Sorry." Mihran quickly folded the paper. "I didn't expect to see you. Did I forget something?"

"I haven't heard from you since the picnic," she said. "So I thought I'd try to talk you into an early movie. Maybe followed by dinner. *Roman Holiday* is playing at the Warner. I'll buy the popcorn, but you're on your own if you want extra butter."

"Sounds great." He grabbed her by the arm and started toward the house. "I'll tell mom she's eating alone tonight."

A copy of the *Fresno Bee* rested on the porch step.

"You steal your neighbor's newspaper?" Teresa asked.

"I picked up a copy at Gideon's on the way home." Mihran tucked the second paper under his arm with the first.

"Couldn't wait to see a box score?"

59

"Sometimes I like to read the paper on my walk home." Mihran held the door open for her. "It helps to pass the time."

***

He was even more distracted and distant on their walk to the theater. There were no questions about her day. No lessons about history or culture that their walks through Armenian Town usually provoked. She considered several ways to ask what he was thinking, but each conversation she played out in her head tended toward an unpleasant ending. So she acquiesced to his silence and turned her attention to the neighborhood.

Most of the homes were small, built decades earlier when two bedrooms and a single bath were as much as any working family could hope for. The lawns were as green as a Fresno summer would allow, the porches cramped with planter boxes, bicycles and mismatched wooden chairs. But the streets were surprisingly alive. Men carried lunch boxes home from work, couples gathered in the shade of front-lawn trees, women tended to vegetable gardens. A dozen boys with a rubber ball and a broom stick played a variation of baseball in the middle of the paved road. People she didn't know waved as they passed. Teresa smiled and waved back.

When they crossed Ventura and entered the tree-lined streets of downtown, she thought of a new tactic to pull him back from wherever he was.

"Can I be nosy?" Teresa asked.

"Whose business do you want to nose into?"

"Your mother's. How has she been able to keep the house and pay for everything since your father passed away?"

"I pretty much take care of the household expenses," Mihran said. "Groceries, utilities. That sort of thing. After all, I live there. I shouldn't expect free room and board."

"So you make the house payments?"

"Nosy *and* direct."

"Two traits that go well together," she said. "Besides, when I become Mrs. Mihran Saropian, don't you think I should be let in on your financial matters?"

"Actually, that's not the way it works in my family."

"The men make all the decisions about money?"

"That's the tradition."

"And what about this generation?" she asked. "Doesn't Serena know about Arak's finances?"

"I doubt if she has any idea what Arak makes," he said. "He gives her cash for expenses. And a weekly allowance."

"Doesn't she ask?"

"Probably not."

"But that's your brother. You would share information about money with your wife. Wouldn't you?"

"Of course."

"Correct answer." Teresa nodded. "So, back to my question. Do you make the house payments?"

"I don't," Mihran said. "And, before you ask, my mother doesn't have any house payments."

"How is that possible?"

"Uncle Henry took care of it," Mihran said. "After my father died, Henry took over the mortgage."

"That was generous."

"I don't really think of it as generosity."

"Then what is it?"

"Family," Mihran said. "Henry's brother died, leaving him with a widowed sister-in-law and two fatherless nephews. Arak and I are the only link to the next generation of Saropians. You saw the family plot. Enough room for four or five generations. That's how Henry sees things."

They entered the heart of downtown Fresno, and suddenly the sidewalks were filled with other young couples. Window shoppers held hands in front of store displays. Lively conversations and the clatter of dishes spewed out of open restaurant doors.

"Serena said Arak was acting secretive last night," Teresa said.

"Since when are you chummy with Serena?"

"I had coffee with your mother and the girls today."

"Oh?"

"I came by to return the picnic dishes. Your mother asked me to stay."

A thin woman in a blue uniform sat inside the ticket booth in front of the theater. Color posters on both sides of the breezeway announced upcoming shows.

"I don't suppose you know what Arak is up to," Teresa said.

"Arak is involved in a lot of things." Mihran bought two tickets, and they joined the line of couples moving toward the door. "Picking season is never easy. And this year there's been some trouble with the workers."

"But none of that is secret."

Mihran handed the tickets to a teenager wearing a gold jacket. The boy tore the tickets in half, dropped one set of stubs through the slot in the top of a red and chrome ticket stand and handed the other set back to Mihran.

"You think Arak is doing something in secret?" Mihran asked.

"Is he?"

"If Arak has secrets, what makes you think I would know about them?"

"Serena said you met with Henry and Arak last night."

Mihran stopped in the middle of the lobby and turned to face her. "It's nothing you need to know about. Really."

"Because I'm not family? Or because I'm a woman?"

"Please." Mihran smiled at her in a way that said he didn't have the strength for a lengthy discussion. "Trust me on this."

"I'm just trying to figure out where the boundaries are. That's all."

"I'm sorry."

"Come on." She grabbed his arm. "Let's see what Gregory Peck and Audrey Hepburn are up to."

Chapter Ten

The movie helped. Or maybe it was just being with Teresa. Halfway through the film, Mihran could feel himself starting to relax. It was, he knew, only a temporary reprieve. A fist momentarily loosening its grip. But for now, it was a moment to savor.

He reached for Teresa's hand as they left the theater, and the sensation of her smooth palm against his made Mihran realize that he had forgotten this simple gesture of affection on their walk downtown.

"Sorry about earlier tonight," Mihran said. "I was a little preoccupied."

"No kidding," Teresa said. "You want to talk about it?"

"I'd rather not bore you."

Teresa expressed her skepticism with a few seconds of silence. "Then can we talk about the picnic yesterday?"

"I was going to call you, wasn't I?"

"That's what you said."

"How many apologies can a man make in one night before he reaches the limit?"

"I'll let you know when you get there."

He reassured her that she had done fine at the picnic, that everyone had liked her, and that she would never again have to spend so much time under the microscope. He also understood that she would probably need to hear the message over and over. Teresa asked him what he thought of the movie, and he had to confess that he had been too distracted to pay much attention.

"I guess sometimes I think too much," Mihran said.

"Perhaps."

"Perhaps? Don't you believe I'm capable of deep thought?"

"Of course you are," Teresa said. "But sometimes you don't stop at rational thinking."

"Are you saying I'm irrational?"

"I think you're willing to go beyond being rational. Like that business with the ghosts at the cemetery."

"You think I see ghosts?"

"I think you might be open to the concept."

"Open-mindedness is a good thing, isn't it?"

"To a point."

"Cemeteries do strange things to people," he said. "A lot of folks are afraid to go near them."

"Exactly. Reason taking a back seat to emotion. The old heart over head."

"And you prefer it the other way around?"

"I don't believe in anything I can't experience."

They passed the Chevrolet showroom. Although the business was closed for the night, the lights remained on. A young couple stood side-by-side in front of the window considering the shiny new cars on display. Without warning, a twinge of dread shot through Mihran. A flash of an image — broken glass and crumpled bodies – came and went. He took a deep breath and reminded himself to focus. Concentrate on each step, on each movement. On acting as if nothing were wrong. The tense moment passed.

"Do you believe in love?" Mihran squeezed Teresa's hand.

"Of course."

"But you'd have to agree that love is not very rational."

"I can experience love. That makes it real."

"Head or heart?" he asked. "Which part of my anatomy do you suppose I was using when I fell for you? My head thinks I should do an analysis. Calculate the pluses and the minuses. Determine logically if I made the right decision to fall in love with this particular individual."

Mihran stopped in the middle of the sidewalk and pinched his chin. "Let's see. Brains. Ambition. Charm. I suppose those would be assets."

He drew an imaginary chart in the air with his finger and added three exaggerated check marks. "Non-Armenian. Oooh. That's probably a negative." Another check mark. "What else? Spends her time with a college student who probably will take forever to finish his degree and doesn't know what he wants to do after graduation. Well, that certainly shows poor judgment."

He took a step back and focused his gaze upon her. "Physical attributes. How should we evaluate her physical appearance?"

Teresa responded by putting her hands on her hips and doing her best to strike a pin-up pose.

"Most definitely a plus," Mihran said. "If fact, we're going to have to add quite a few points to this side of the ledger."

Mihran made several check marks on his imaginary chart. Teresa relaxed her pose.

"Wait, wait, wait." Mihran said. "I'm not through evaluating that last feature."

Teresa wrapped both arms around him. "I concede the point. Sometimes heart wins out over head."

She pressed the side of her face against his chest. He closed his eyes and allowed the honey and citrus fragrance of her hair to envelope his senses. Dozens of faceless people passed by as time and place became irrelevant, and soon they were swaying together to a silent rhythm. He held her as if clinging to a life preserver, and for the first time in the past 24 hours, Mihran entertained the thought that somehow the fears now perched on the edges of his awareness would be defeated.

Later that night, when they were lying side by side in the darkness of her bedroom, Teresa returned to the conversation.

"Not being Armenian. Is that really a negative?" She spoke the words while lying on her back.

"Not for me."

"But for some people. Your brother doesn't like it."

"He just needs a little time."

"And your mother?"

"In case you hadn't noticed, she's crazy about you."

"What about your Uncle Henry?"

"She's not as crazy about him."

Teresa poked him in the side. "Come on, this is important."

"OK," Mihran said. "Speaking rationally, I think you're kind of a threat."

"A threat to what?"

"A way of life."

"Armenian men in Fresno have always married non-Armenians," she said. "You told me that yourself."

"Those women married into the whole package," he said. "They joined the church. They learned to cook Armenian food. Some of them even learned the language."

"Is that what you want?"

"You know I don't," he said. "And if I did, we both know that I'd have to find a new girlfriend."

Mihran glanced at the objects in her room, identified now only by their silvery outlines. Teresa found safety here, especially in the darkness. This was where they held their most intimate conversations, where she waited to pose the delicate questions that came to her during the day.

"Does your mother ever talk about what happened to her back then?" Teresa asked. "Back in Armenia?"

"Not often."

"Is the topic off-limits?"

"I wouldn't say that," Mihran said. "It's just an understanding that's always been there. We talk about those things in general. But not about her experiences specifically."

"Because she'd rather not remember?"

"Actually, it's something none of us ever wants to forget."

"Who is us?"

"I was thinking of the Saropians. But every family has a story."

"At what point do they let it go?" she asked.

"Why should they let it go?"

"I mean, how many generations have to carry the burden?"

"Maybe that's why you're a threat," he said. "If the community breaks up, who would do the remembering? Who would tell the stories?"

"Would that be so bad? To move on?"

"And what would you say to the victims?" he asked. "How could you tell them that they died for nothing?"

"Why do they have to die for something?"

"Because thinking the opposite is unacceptable."

"What are you saying? That everything happens for some purpose?"

"Not exactly," he said. "But I do believe in right and wrong."

"That no bad deed goes unpunished? That eventually justice will be done?"

"It's not that simple. But something like that."

"Where's the justice in what happened to your mother?"

"Maybe we haven't seen the final outcome."

"You think the killers will be punished in the afterlife?" she asked. "Is that how you make sense of tragedy?"

"I wouldn't say that either."

"So what's the answer?"

"I don't have the answer," he said. "But I think those of us who know the story, I think it's up to us to keep the memories alive. As long as people know what happened — if we keep telling the stories — then maybe some good can come out of it."

"Is that what they taught you growing up?" she asked.

"More or less," he said. "But the truth is, I didn't really spend much time thinking about these things. Not until I was in the army."

"That's something you never talk about."

"What don't I talk about?"

"The army."

"I told you. I was in Korea."

"But we've never had a conversation about that."

"No reason to."

"How could it not be interesting?" Teresa asked. "I don't need to hear war stories. But an experience like that would have to have an impact on a person."

"It's something I did," Mihran said. "It's not who I am."

"Can I ask why you don't want to talk about it?"

"I don't know what to tell you. I was in the army. Like a lot of guys. There was a war. I did my duty."

"Did you see combat?"

"Combat is part of war."

A quiet moment passed.

"Did you ever kill anyone?" she asked.

"You said you didn't want to hear war stories."

"I want to hear stories about you."

"There are no stories about me," he said. "You do what you're told. Someone else makes the decisions. You're just the tool."

"Still, it has to affect you."

"It's not a big deal. OK?"

She fell silent, and Mihran knew they were thinking the same thing. His reaction betrayed his words when said it wasn't important.

"So what do you want to know?" he asked.

"Was it bad?"

"At times."

"Most of the time?"

"Occasionally."

"Do you think about it?"

"Not too often."

"But sometimes," she said. "And is it painful to think about? Are you haunted by it?"

"I wouldn't say that."

Teresa rolled onto her side so she could face him. "So did you?"

"Did I what?"

"Kill someone?"

"Would it matter?" he asked. "Would you disapprove?"

"It was war. I understand."

"No, you don't."

"I'm not judging you."

"Of course, you are," he said. "I judge myself. I would expect you to do the same."

She granted him a quiet moment to gather his thoughts.

"You want to know if I killed anyone in Korea?" he asked.

"If you want to tell me."

"The truth is, I don't know."

"I don't understand."

"It's not like you're standing right in front of them," he said. "You shoot, you take cover. You try not to get yourself killed."

Mihran turned his body away. It was easier to find the words when he was not looking at her.

"I shot at enemy soldiers," he said. "Or in the direction of enemy soldiers."

Teresa waited.

"You want to hear a story? One story?"

"If you want to tell me one."

"Two weeks before my tour was up," he said. "I was separated a little from my unit. I could see they were being fired on from above. Then for a second. Maybe it wasn't even a second. I see one of them.

Just his head. He stood to throw a grenade in the general direction of my unit. Then he ducked out of sight again. No one was hurt, but I knew where he was. So I sprayed the area."

"What happened?"

"The firing stopped. I sprayed the area with bullets, and then nothing. We pulled back. We never went up there to see."

She placed a hand gently on his shoulder.

"I used my rifle many times in the war," he said. "But that was the only time I ever got a clear look at the face of a man I shot at."

"You know, it's OK if you did."

"I know."

"It was war. You had no choice."

"That's right."

"A lot of soldiers did the same thing."

"Then I guess it must be all right."

Mihran stared into the dark room, connected to Teresa by the hand on his shoulder and the sound of her breathing.

"There's probably a man about my age somewhere in China or Korea," he said. "A man who shot at me once. Maybe he lies in bed at night wondering if he killed me."

"Too bad you can't tell him."

"Maybe it's better that he doesn't know," Mihran said. "Keeps him wondering. Keeps him thinking. Maybe that's not all bad."

Chapter Eleven

It had been many years since Henry had actually enjoyed himself in a *surjaran*, if he ever had. When he was young, unmarried Armenian men in the valley outnumbered single Armenian women by at least two to one. An evening at the coffeehouse was an evening not spent alone.

The Asbarez Club had changed little in four decades. The room was filled with dozens of men sipping coffee, smoking cigarettes and playing cards. Groups of regulars came to own certain tables, and those who skipped an evening were asked about. For Henry, what had once been an escape from loneliness eventually became a place for making contacts. He had recognized early on that a successful business was built handshake by handshake, conversation by conversation. There was no better place for a Fresno Armenian to build that foundation than the Asbarez Club.

He scanned faces until he found Babeg Bedrosian and Dikran Kachigian hunched over a small table in the far corner.

"My friends." Henry smiled as he approached.

"Your place is waiting for you." Babeg pushed an empty chair away from the table and motioned for Henry to sit.

"A little late this evening," Dikran said. "Something important going on?"

"There's never enough time during picking season," Henry said.

"I guess we're lucky you could come at all," Dikran said.

A boy Henry recognized as the owner's nephew approached to take his order. Table service was a courtesy limited to the senior patrons of the *surjaran*. The boy, no older than 15, was tall and gangly with a neck that seemed too long to support the weight of his head.

"Coffee, please," Henry said.

"Another for me as well." Babeg held his empty cup at eye level to make his point.

"I am not yet ready for more coffee." Dikran spoke in Armenian, although the boy had asked for their orders in English. "But tell me, young man. Do you have *banirov boereg?*"

A confused expression spread across the boy's face. "I'm sorry, sir."

Dikran sighed then repeated the words slowly. The boy nodded when he recognized the name of the pastry.

"I have learned several languages in my lifetime," Dikran said after the boy left with their orders. "Including English. Why is it so much trouble for the young ones to learn the language of their ancestors?"

"Times are changing," Babeg said. "That's for sure."

"It's a different generation," Henry said. "Most of them were born in this country. They're as much American as they are Armenian."

"And then what?" Dikran said. "*Their* children will be more American than Armenian? And after that, not even Armenian at all? The language is the first thing to go."

"Remember that guy who used come here?" Babeg said. "What was his name? Toutikian? He had that red mark on the side of his face. Looked like a big red bell right on the side of his face. You'd see him in here all the time."

"Tourikian," Henry said. "Misak Tourikian."

"That's him," Babeg said. "Remember how he used to talk? He was always saying how he was moving back to Armenia someday. Said we all should go. Return to the homeland. He talked about it all the time."

"That was 25 years ago," Henry said. "The time for going back to the old country has passed."

"There you are," Dikran said. "Not even a homeland to return to. And a generation that would rather their ancestors came over on the Mayflower. Look around. Our culture is on its death bed."

"When I look around, I see a room full of Armenian men," Henry said. "Young Armenian men. And at Holy Trinity on Sunday, I see young families with children. The same families I see at the picnics. They eat shish kabob. They dance the *tamzara.*"

"There are more Armenians in Fresno now than there ever were," Babeg said.

"Next picnic, take a closer look," Dikran said. "A lot of those Armenian men are with their *odar* wives. And their children – some of them don't look Armenian at all. I see blond hair on some of those kids."

"Armenian men in Fresno have always married *odar* women," Henry said. "Have you forgotten what it was like when we were young?"

"Tamar Donabedian's boy," Dikran said. "He married an *odar* last year. Then moved to Sanger. Now he calls himself Donabed. Stephen Donabed. They say it was his wife's idea. She doesn't want people to think maybe *she's* Armenian."

"I suppose this is where you complain about the names everyone's giving their children," Henry said.

Dikran lifted his cup to his lips before answering. A roar came from a nearby table where a game of *tavlu* had apparently come to an exciting finish.

"I remember when Henry was Hagop," Dikran said to Babeg. "His mother rented a house on L Street. A little place with a garden in front. Ana Saropian. Ana and little Hagop used to sell tomatoes and peppers right there on the porch. Sometimes Hagop's little brother Bedros would help. Ana Saropian. She was Ana all her life. And Bedros was always Bedros. God rest their souls."

"And I am still Hagop," Henry said. "I will always be Hagop. And my gravestone will say Hagop."

"But these *odars* you work with," Dikran said. "They want to do business with Henry. Not with Hagop."

"If they would rather deal with someone named Henry, what's the harm?"

"I'm sure they are very respectful to you," Dikran said.

"With a few exceptions, yes," Henry said. "You would be surprised how respectful people are when you have something they want."

Dikran reached for his cup again but stopped short when he saw the long-necked boy approach with their orders.

"And when you are not doing business," Dikran said. "What do you suppose these people say about Armenians? I mean, when you are not around."

"I would have no way of knowing," Henry said.

"How soon we forget," Dikran said.

"What do you even know about the world outside of Armenian Town?" Henry asked. "How would you know what *odars* are thinking?"

"For 35 years, I sold fabrics for Aram Aberian," Dikran said. "Every *odar* who came into the shop was the same. *You can't trust an Armenian.* They said it to our faces. Some would count their change right in front of me. *Armenians will cheat you out of every cent they can,* they'd say. They left no doubt about how they felt about us."

"Like that supplier who sold you the needles and thread," Babeg said.

"That's exactly what I'm talking about," Dikran said. "I asked this *odar,* 'How much you want for the thread?' I would have paid a fair price. But he turns to his partner and says, 'These Armenians, always pinching pennies.' Then he turns to me and says, 'Why don't you just tell me right now how little you are going to offer me, so we can save some time?'"

Henry had heard story many times, which Dikran obviously knew. If he had his way, they would change the topic. But Dikran had forced his hand.

"Back in Armenia," Henry said, "there were no set prices for crops or material. People worked with one another to come to a fair price for everyone."

"That sure doesn't happen here," Babeg said.

"The first Armenians in the valley tried to do the same as they did back home," Henry said. "We were simply bartering. But the people here thought we were being miserly."

"So it was all a misunderstanding." Dikran waved his hand in a dismissive fashion. "If we would stop bartering, there would be no more distrust and suspicion. The *odars* would flock to our stores. They would beg us to move next door to them."

"We all know the sting of hatred," Henry said. "But answer me this. How are you going to make things change? By retreating into your own world? By letting the *odars* continue to believe about us what they want? Or by showing them that they are wrong?"

"There is a reason we live in Armenian Town," Dikran said. "Do you believe the *odars* will welcome us now just because the laws have changed? Ask Babeg what happened last year when his cousin tried to buy a house in an *odar* neighborhood."

"They sold it to somebody else," Babeg said. "Gaspar made his bid first. But they waited until they got another bid from an *odar* and sold it to them. For the same amount of money. Exactly the same."

"People don't give you respect just because you want them to," Henry said. "You have to earn it. With the *odars*, you have to beat them at their own game."

"Is that what you are doing?" Dikran said. "Then tell me, my friend. Now that you have earned their respect, how many of these businessmen you deal with during the day invite you into their home in the evening?"

"Ask yourself this," Henry said. "At the end of the transaction, who has the money in his pocket?"

"Money," Dikran said. "Of course. It's always about money."

"It's what people understand," Henry said. "You get their attention and, in due time, you get their respect. *If* you have the money."

"You see how you have adopted their standards?" Dikran said. "I wonder if you would be talking like this if we were in Armenia."

"The Soviets wouldn't let you," Babeg said. "Nobody has any more money than anyone else now that the communists have taken over."

"You can spend your whole life dreaming about the way things were," Henry said. "Or you can do something about the way things are."

The conversation was interrupted when Arak appeared at the table.

"I thought I might find you here," Arak said.

"Please join us," Babeg said.

"No, thank you," Arak said. "I just wanted to let Henry know that I'm back. Wanted to see if there's anything going on that I should know about."

"You take a trip, Arak?" Babeg said. "Where'd you go?"

"Just down south," Arak said. "Just one night."

"A trip in the middle of picking season?" Dikran said. "Must have been pretty important."

"I don't believe you missed anything," Henry said.

"Well, that's good news, then." Arak nodded to Babeg and Dikran. "Sorry to interrupt. Enjoy the rest of your evening."

"Someone was looking for you," Dikran said.

"For me?" Arak asked.

"A policeman." Dikran took a bite of pastry. "That Armenian boy."

"Anaforian?"

"That's the one. He was in here earlier tonight."

Arak curled his fingers around the top of the empty chair. "And he was looking for me?"

"He was asking if anyone had seen you," Dikran said. "I guess he didn't know you were out of town."

"Probably something to do with the pickers," Arak said.

"You got trouble with the Mexicans?" Babeg asked.

"The usual," Arak said. "Stuff disappearing. Happens every year."

"He was asking about the Turks," Dikran said.

"What Turks?" Arak said.

"The ones at the picnic," Dikran said. "You know, the ones you told to leave."

"Well," Arak said. "Anaforian knows how to find me."

Henry waited until Arak was gone. "You did not mention the police officer earlier, Dikran."

"He was asking about Arak, not you," Dikran said. "Is there some reason you are interested in this business between Arak and the police?"

"If it's about the farm and the pickers," Henry said, "then I think I should know what's going on."

"Arak leaves town in the middle of picking season, and then the police want to talk with him." Dikran took a long sip of coffee. "I suppose if I were you, I would want to know what was going on myself."

Chapter Twelve

Arak sat in the chair his uncle had occupied two nights earlier and took measure of the two police officers sitting across from him. They had been waiting outside his home. One man was certainly his enemy. He wore a blue suit and had introduced himself only as Officer Logan. He leaned forward on the edge of the seat and kept his eyes focused on Arak. The other man was harder to gauge. Ricky Anaforian wore his police uniform, his hat resting on his lap. His presence was no coincidence. Anaforian was the first and still the only Armenian in the Fresno Police Department. For as long as Arak could remember, people referred to Anaforian only by his last name. He was a few years older than Arak, had grown up in the neighborhood and had married an Armenian girl, Kelly Abrahamian. But last year they moved into an apartment out on Butler, more than a mile from Armenian Town. And it seemed to Arak that Anaforian didn't come to the picnics or church events as often as he used to.

"Mr. Saropian." Logan held a thin notebook in one hand, a pencil in the other. His slim black tie hung between his knees. "Were you at the picnic in Kingsburg on Sunday? The picnic at Oakwood Park?"

"Sure. We always go."

"Do you recall if anything out of the ordinary happened there?"

"I guess you're talking about the Turks."

"You want to tell me about that?"

"Not much to tell," Arak said. "A group of Turks came by the picnic. I guess they didn't realize it was an Armenian event. So me and some other guys told them they should leave."

"What other guys?"

"I don't remember exactly. A bunch of men. Maybe six or seven of us."

"And what did the Turks say when you told them to leave?" Logan asked.

"At first they didn't seem to understand what the problem was."

"Why would there be a problem?"

"It's an Armenian activity," Arak said. "There's a history between Armenians and Turks."

"Are you saying you don't like Turks?"

"Ask your Armenian officer there." Arak nodded toward Anaforian. "We got good reason to not like Turks."

Logan kept his eyes on Arak. Of course, he and Anaforian would have discussed all of this beforehand.

"How many Turks were at the picnic?" Logan asked.

"Five that I saw. Three guys and two girls."

"Did you say anything else to these Turks, besides asking them to leave?"

"We exchanged a few words."

"And what words were those?"

"I don't remember exactly," Arak said. "I just made it clear to them that they weren't welcome."

"So there was an argument."

"I wouldn't call it an argument."

"Did you threaten them? Tell them to leave or something might happen?"

"I just made it clear that they should go. They were outnumbered, you know? So what would be the point of them arguing?"

"Outnumbered? Sounds like they might have felt threatened."

"I didn't hear anybody threaten anybody," Arak said. "Can I ask what this is all about?"

"When did you leave the picnic?" Logan asked.

Arak paused as if searching his memory. "Somewhere between 6:30 and 7:00, I guess."

"Did you drive home with your family?"

"I drove with my brother Mihran."

"Your car? You were driving?"

"Yes and yes."

"Anyone else in the car?" Logan asked.

"Just the two of us."

"You come straight home?"

"We stopped at Vincent's to buy cigarettes," Arak said. "You know, the little grocery on the highway."

"Did you see anyone at Vincent's?"

"Just Vincent."

"You see anyone in the parking lot as you were coming or going?"

"Not that I remember."

"So after you left the store, you drove down 99?" Logan asked. "Then turned onto Clovis Avenue?"

"Right."

"Did you see anything unusual as you drove down Clovis?"

"No." Arak drew out the answer as if he were doing his best to remember.

"There was an accident on Clovis Avenue that night," Logan said. "Around the time you would have been driving in the area. Were you aware of that?"

"It must have happened after we came through."

"A car ran off the road. Hit a tree. Two people were hurt."

"I'm sorry to hear that."

"They were two of the Turks you chased out of the picnic," Logan said. "That seem like a coincidence to you?"

"I don't know what to make of it," Arak said. "I hope they're OK."

Logan stared at his notebook before continuing. He had yet to write anything down.

"I'm going to ask you flat out," Logan said. "Do you know anything about that accident out on Clovis Avenue last Sunday?"

"Only what I've learned just now from you."

"And you're saying you and your brother drove straight home and had nothing to do with the Turks after the picnic?"

"We stopped at Vincent's."

"And then straight home? Without seeing the Turks or their car?"

"Yes." Arak nodded. "That's exactly what happened."

Logan and Anaforian exchanged glances.

"I guess that's all for now." Logan rose to his feet.

Arak escorted the two policemen to the door. Logan thanked Arak for his time and said something about maybe coming back for more questions at a later date. Arak watched from the open door as they made their way to the street. Just before stepping into the passenger side of the car, Anaforian glanced back at Arak and gave an almost imperceptible nod. Arak returned the gesture and closed the door. Everything was going to be all right.

Chapter Thirteen

Henry could not be sure of the time, but it most likely was past eleven. A nearly full moon had risen over the Sierras hours earlier. He turned the Cadillac down a dirt road that cut through the middle of several acres of almond trees. The road came to an abrupt end a couple of hundred feet into the orchard. He turned the engine and then the headlights off, which caused the trees to disappear momentarily until his eyes adjusted to the faint light. Moonlight cast purple and gray shadows over the entire scene.

He found a pack of cigarettes in the glove compartment and opened the car's window before lighting one. As often happened during these night visits, his thoughts turned to his father. Sirak Saropian had worked in this very orchard when it belonged to a man named Anderson. One day, seven-year-old Hagob joined his father. Sirak showed him how to spread the large canvas under the trees and how to beat the trunks with soft mallets until all the ripe almonds were knocked out of the branches. They started early in the day, but within a few hours the August sun beat down on them whenever they stepped from under the shade of the trees. By afternoon, the heat consumed Hagob's energy and left the boy a little lightheaded. He was covered with the dust, dead leaves and cobwebs that fell from the trees along with the almonds. Rivers of perspiration formed lines on his dirty face and arms and stung his eyes.

Anderson was a thin man who stared at his workers with penetrating blue eyes. He walked among the rows, checking to see that bags were full and that each tree was empty before the workers moved on to the next. "Don't leave my almonds for the squirrels," he yelled. "I'll get some Mexicans in here who'll clean those trees if you can't."

At the end of the day, Hagob and Sirak lined up with the others

81

to receive their pay. Anderson sat at a small table in the shade of a maple tree adding numbers and handing out cash. Hagob stood behind his father and watched the exchanges as each man made his way to the front of the line. They all stood a respectable distance from the table and spoke in soft tones.

"Name?" Anderson demanded when Sirak approached.

"Saropian."

Anderson followed his finger down a sheet of paper filled with names and numbers. "Says here 34. You look awfully small for someone who claims he can fill 34 bags in one day."

"My son helped." Sirak gestured toward Hagob. "We put the family name on our bags."

Anderson studied the boy for a second. His eyes did not blink. Hagob looked away.

"I seen some of those bags of yours. You call them full?"

Sirak did not answer. Hagob knew they had filled their bags as high or higher than the workers around them.

"They don't pay me for almonds by the bag," Anderson said. "They pay me by the pound. You're going to cost me money if I pay you for 34 bags." Anderson opened his metal cash box and studied the contents for a moment. "I'll pay you for 30, and that's being generous. If you can't do better for me tomorrow, don't bother coming back."

Anderson set the cash on the table between them. Sirak kept his arms to his side for a few seconds as if considering the amount. Then Hagob watched his father pick up the money.

"Thank you, sir," Sirak said.

Years later, long after Sirak's death, Henry had saved enough money to start buying land of his own. Anderson's farm was the first piece of property he acquired.

"No one takes advantage of a man with money," Henry said aloud. He finished his cigarette and tossed the butt out the window. "You see, father? We have beaten them at their own game."

Chapter Fourteen

The first person Arak saw when he drove into Saropian Farms the next morning was Leon Nazarian. Leon sat in the dirt, his back against the office door. He leapt to his feet when Arak stepped from the car.

"Oh man. Oh man." Leon's hair stuck out in all directions, and his eyes had a way of locking onto whoever he was talking to. "It's good you're here. Things been goin' to hell. Goin' straight to hell."

"What sorts of things?" Arak asked.

"Man, oh man." Leon pursed his lips and clenched his fists as he worked to gather his thoughts.

Everyone was patient with Leon. He had spent most of the second World War as a prisoner of war, miraculously surviving the Bataan Death March and war camps in the Philippines and Japan. Permanent red and purple splotches on the left side of his face attested to the beatings he had endured in captivity. The blows had left him with what people politely called an unpredictable mind. After the war, Leon had been hired and fired from a dozen jobs until Henry took him on as a farmhand. Leon could disappear for days at a time, and his work often had to be done again by one of the other farmhands. But he had sacrificed for his country. And his loyalty to Henry and Saropian Farms was never in question.

"Over in the north vineyard," Leon said. "A whole row of grapes. Someone walked right down the middle of a whole row of picked grapes. More than a hundred trays. Stomped right in the middle of every one."

"Can we save anything?"

"Not much," Leon said. "The son-of-a-bitch stomped two or three times on most of 'em. They'd only been on the ground a day or two. Ruined the whole damned row. The whole damned row."

"It's something every year with these pickers." Arak moved toward his office door.

Leon shifted his weight from foot to foot. He had more to say. Arak pretended to busy himself with his keys while he waited.

"We also got some stuff missing," Leon blurted out.

"I keep telling everyone, we've got to keep the tools locked up during picking season."

"Not tools," Leon said. "Some of those crates. The ones we stacked by the side of the barn. The ones we use for shipping the raisins."

"How many crates?"

"Ten, or maybe even more. But we found them."

"You found the thieves or you found the crates?"

"Kenny found a pile of burnt-up wood over near the pond," Leon said. "He showed me. They was the crates. You could see Saropian markings on some of them. On the parts that weren't completely burned."

"Burnt like in a campfire?"

"Not a campfire." Leon squinted into the distance as if picturing the burnt crates. "More like someone just throwed them crates in a pile and lit them on fire. There was no order to it, not like you would with a campfire. And it didn't look like anyone had been sitting around or anything."

"You think someone took our crates just so they could burn them?"

"That's what Kenny was saying," Leon said. "It's got to be the Mexicans. But you can't watch them all the time."

"I'll check it out myself this morning. Anything else?"

"That's all I know. But you can never tell with them people."

Arak slapped Leon on the shoulder. "Good work."

Leon could not hold back a grin.

"Keep an eye on things as best you can, Leon." Arak turned his attention back to the office door. "And let me know if anything else disappears."

"Yes, sir."

The door opened but a few inches before banging into something. Arak forced it fully open then paused to survey the room before entering. A granite rock nearly a foot across rested on the floor among broken glass. The window just above the desk was shattered. Shards of glass littered the desktop.

"Now what?" Arak lifted the rock and assessed the weight. It would have taken two hands to toss it through the high window.

"Oh, Lord." Leon leaned through the open door but did not enter. His eyes widened. "Who did this?"

"Same ones who stomped the grapes and burned the crates." Arak took a towel from the corner wash basin and brushed the glass from his chair.

"The sons-a-bitches." Leon leaned forward and lifted a small piece of glass. He studied it as if there were answers to be found in the shard.

"You got that right." Arak stepped to the shattered window. Even in daylight, anyone could have come and gone unseen through the rows of vines that ran behind the building.

"Why would anyone do such a thing?" Leon said. "What the hell were they thinking?"

"They're trying to scare me, Leon," Arak said. "But that's where they made their mistake."

"You want me to clean up?"

"Use the broom in the barn," Arak said. "And I'd rather you didn't tell anyone about the broken window. OK?"

"You know I won't."

"I do know that, Leon." Arak looked his farmhand in the eye and nodded. "When push comes to shove, people have to take sides."

Arak set the rock on top of his desk. Stealing he understood, even expected. The destroyed grapes and the burnt crates could be dismissed as acts of anger directed toward the farm or maybe toward whoever happened to own the property. But the rock through the window. This was something new.

Chapter Fifteen

Mihran waited for cars to pass before darting across Fulton Avenue and into the shade provided by the downtown buildings. It was three o'clock – the hottest part of the day – and the early September heat had not yet broken. He loosened the tie Jack insisted he wear in the office.

Gideon nodded toward the stack of *Fresno Bees* as Mihran approached. "Got here no more than five minutes ago."

"Looks like I've become predictable." Mihran grabbed a newspaper, set his nickel on the counter, and glanced though the headlines as he headed to the courthouse. There was nothing about the accident. No news at all since the short article on Monday. He tossed the paper into the first trash can he saw.

The marbled hallways of the courthouse offered a cool respite from the heat. Mihran's business in the records office was completed in a matter of minutes, but the prospect of spending the rest of the afternoon behind his desk was more than he was ready to face. On days like this, Jack's two rotating fans did little more than scatter untethered papers.

Mihran made his way to the first-floor courtroom. If he was lucky, there would be a trial, and he could slip inside and watch a few minutes of the proceedings. The show never failed to fascinate him. He had been watching snippets of trials for more than a year, and, by his own account, had become quite adept at reading people's emotions. Attorneys, defendants, the judge, jurors, witnesses, family members and even the occasional news reporter were all on display. Boredom was the most common expression, especially in the judges. But it was not difficult to find fear, confusion, anger and, occasionally, pity. Mihran also liked the rigid lines and right angles that defined the physical structure of the courtroom. He appreciated the way tables for each side were positioned to reflect equal access to the bench. And how the judge, the personification of justice, sat calculatingly higher than everyone else.

But today the large walnut doors to the courtroom stood open to reveal an empty chamber. Mihran settled onto a bench across from the open doors. Five more minutes, he told himself. Surely he was entitled to a short break before returning to the hot office. He allowed his eyes to close and, despite the hard wooden bench, and was not at all sure that he would not fall asleep.

As he enjoyed the cool and calm, Mihran gradually became aware of a conversation between two approaching men. One voice was high-pitched and full of energy, the other slow and reflective.

"It's not a matter of right or wrong," the man with the patient voice said. "It's a matter of evidence and what we can prove."

"What am I to do?" The second man spoke with a heavy accent. Eastern European. Polish perhaps, or maybe Hungarian. "I have been cheated. I have lost nearly everything."

"I'm giving you my best advice. That's what you pay me for. And I have to tell you, as things stand now, I don't see a case."

"So I am left with nothing? Where is the justice in that?"

"There's justice, and then there's the law."

"So he gets away with it? He takes my money, and I can do nothing about it?"

"I know it doesn't sound right. But, yes. That's what I've been telling you. That's the system. Sometimes the right guy wins, and sometimes he doesn't."

Mihran listened to the final exchanges and the sound of one man's footsteps disappearing down the tiled hallway. When he opened his eyes, he saw the rounded shoulders of the remaining man silhouetted in the open doorway. The man's jacket was too small for him, and his shoes were scuffed and worn. He stared into the empty courtroom with a posture depleted of purpose. It was the pose of a defeated man.

Mihran rose to leave, but the scraping of his feet against the tile startled the man. He turned and stared at Mihran as if surprised to see anyone else in the building.

"You." He pointed toward Mihran. "Are you a lawyer?"

"I'm afraid not."

The man looked at Mihran as if he did not believe him. "You are on trial? Maybe arrested?"

"Nothing like that," Mihran said. "I do work for a lawyer. But I'm just a college student."

"Then you want to be a lawyer someday?"

"I've thought about it."

"Let me ask you something, college student." The man gestured toward the empty courtroom. "What do you think of this system of yours? Is this the place to find justice?"

"Not always."

"And when the system does not work, how does a man in this country go about finding his justice?"

"I hope you are not thinking about taking the law into your own hands."

"I am not saying anything. I am asking."

"I'll grant you that the system is not perfect."

The man made a scoffing sound. "You sound like someone who has always had the law on his side."

"I'm not sure that's true."

"I was cheated." The man took a step forward. "Cheated out of almost all the money I had. The police say they can do nothing. They say I can sue. But the lawyer, he tells me now that I cannot win if I sue. I cannot get my money back. I am left with nothing. What do you think of that?"

"I think it's terrible." Other answers came to him. But no academic phrases or abstract concepts could ease this man's sense of betrayal.

"Well, good luck, college student." The man turned to go. "Good luck with your system. I hope you find justice. I hope someone does."

Mihran watched the deflated man make his way down the hallway, but the words hung in the air. He stepped to the doorway of the empty courtroom. Yes, the system was flawed. The year and a half he had worked for Jack had put to rest nearly all of his idealized notions of what it meant to have a career in law. But the starting point – the realization that law represented one avenue to overcome injustice – remained with him. It was his high school Government teacher who had first suggested a career in law. Mr. Davenport was no more than five feet tall and constantly in motion. He spoke more rapidly than anyone Mihran had ever met, as if there was not enough time to express everything he needed to say. But when he suggested law school, Mihran could only laugh. An Armenian lawyer? There was no such thing in Fresno. Then do this for me, his teacher had said. Do your class paper on restrictive conveyances. Start with *Shelley vs. Kraemer*, he had said, which came out *Kah-ra-ya-mahr* in his North Carolinian accent.

Mihran would later come to see that it was all a plan. As Mr. Davenport knew it would, reading about restrictive conveyances opened Mihran's eyes. Until the Supreme Court had ruled them illegal just the previous year, deeds commonly included clauses to prevent the sale of homes to specific groups of people, including "undesirables." In Fresno, Mihran learned, undesirables meant Armenians. Armenians had stayed in Armenian Town because legally they had no other place to live.

Although he never checked any box that identified him as a pre-law student, the thought was in the back of Mihran's mind when he took advantage of the GI Bill and enrolled in college. He tried to visit his former teacher shortly after his return from Korea only to discover that Mr. Davenport no longer lived in the area. There were several rumors surrounding his sudden departure. The most persistent was that Mr. Davenport had married a Negro woman and that the two of them had moved to Europe where their relationship was less objectionable. It was a rumor Mihran could not bring himself to believe, but also one he could not completely reject.

***

As he started down the courthouse steps and back into the heat, Mihran was struck by the silence of the afternoon. The park surrounding the courthouse seemed abandoned. Even the retired men who usually filled the shaded benches had been driven inside. The only hint of a breeze came from the leaves that fluttered at the very tops of the oaks and maples.

But the stillness was broken by the sudden appearance of several men and women marching down the main walkway directly toward him. Their collective voices sliced through the empty air. Mihran moved to the edge of the walkway to allow them room to pass.

But they did not pass.

A small man with a thin moustache and angry dark eyes stepped from the group and pointed toward Mihran. "He's one of them."

For a moment, no one seemed to know how to react.

"From the picnic." The accusing man continued to point. "He was one of them that told us to leave. He stood right next to the son-of-a-bitch that said those things to Emin."

The other men in the group began to move in cautious, uncertain steps. Mihran counted five altogether. Twice he stepped to the side, but each time one of the men moved to cut him off. Soon they had formed a circle around him. The women disappeared into the background.

One man stepped forward until he stood a few feet in front of Mihran. He was several inches taller than the others, and his tight pullover shirt highlighted his muscular features. He appeared to be in his twenties, with deep-set eyes and a square face that was almost as wide as it was long.

"Now *you* are the outnumbered one." His dark hair glistened with perspiration. "How brave are you now? What kind of lies would you like to tell us now?"

Mihran raised two open hands in front of him. "I don't want any trouble. I was at the picnic, but I didn't have anything to do with what happened."

"You cannot lie your way out of what you did to Emin and Hazan."

"I'm sorry, but I don't know these people," Mihran said.

"The accident. You ran them off the road."

"I don't know anything about an accident."

"But you are not going to get away with it." The tall man squinted at Mihran, as if taking measure of an opponent. "You and the other murderers are going to prison. All of you. We will see to that."

"Honestly, I don't know what you are talking about."

"Do Armenians do anything but lie?" The man's chest heaved in anger. He clenched his fists but kept them at his side.

A long moment passed. Everyone seemed to be waiting for a signal. Then Mihran felt fingers digging into his shoulder. He spun out of the grip in time to feel a fist fly inches from his chin. A woman screamed.

"You won't get away with it." The voice came from behind Mihran.

"You will pay for what you have done." Another voice, this one from his right.

A flurry of movement and noise followed. Mihran took a blow to the ribs. Then another on the side of the neck. A kick to the knee caused his leg to buckle. He braced himself against the ground with his arm and pushed himself back to his feet. He raised his arms in front of his face and ran toward a sliver of an opening he saw in the circle. A fist caught him in the middle of the back and knocked him onto the cement walkway. He picked himself up, but a blow on the side of the head sent him reeling into a pine tree. Mihran rolled under a low-hanging branch, crawled past the trunk, got to his feet and raced into an open space.

He heard what sounded like a whistle. Without slowing, he looked over his shoulder and saw two policemen. One was standing with arms spread in front of the Turks as if holding back the horde. The other was blowing his whistle and running club-in-hand directly at Mihran.

Mihran stopped. He doubled over and gasped for air.

"What the hell's going on here?" The policeman stopped several feet short of Mihran and raised his club.

"I...was...attacked." Each syllable required a separate breath.

"Why were you attacked?" The policeman wiped perspiration from his forehead. His generous stomach extended over his thick black belt, and he obviously was not pleased about having to exert himself in this heat.

"I don't know. I didn't do anything."

"For no reason at all, they just decided to attack you?"

Mihran looked in the direction of the Turks. The muscular Turk was pointing toward Mihran and thrashing his arms in the air as he spoke to the other officer.

"There was an incident last Sunday." Mihran paused to consider his words. "There was a picnic in Kingsburg. Armenians meet there every week. Last Sunday some Turks showed up. I guess some of these people were part of that group."

"So what happened Sunday that would make these Turks want to come after you?"

"I don't really know," Mihran said. "They were told to leave the picnic. And I guess they're angry about it."

"They want to beat you up because you kicked them out of a picnic?"

"I didn't tell them to leave. Someone else did."

"Who?"

"I'm not sure." ·

"Don't screw around with me." The policeman jabbed his club in Mihran's direction as if brandishing a bayonet. "Give me the whole story right this second, or I'll haul your sorry ass off to jail."

"There's a history of bad blood between Armenians and Turks," Mihran said. "I guess that's part of it."

"But what did you do to piss them off today?"

"Nothing."

"You didn't do a damned thing?"

"I was just walking," Mihran said. "That's the truth. I was on my way back to work."

"Listen to me." The officer wiped his brow again and made no effort to hide the disgust on his face. "You people want to fight each other, go back to the old country and do it. We don't need that around here. You understand?"

"Yes, sir."

The policeman led Mihran to the courthouse steps and told him to sit there while he straightened things out. Although he would have preferred to wait in the shade, Mihran did as he was told.

He took inventory as he watched the two officers talk with the Turks. His right knee was throbbing, and the left side of his face ached. He ran his hand across his cheek and jaw. Already some swelling. A hole in the knee of his pants was soaked with blood. His shirt was torn at the collar. He could only imagine what he looked like to anyone who passed by. With any luck, he would be out of here before anyone he knew saw him.

The policeman returned several minutes later. "We're going to let everybody go this time." He seemed exhausted by the experience.

"Thank you."

"This better be the end of it. We're not going to have this kind of crap in this town. You people want to live here, you're going to act civilized. You understand?"

"Yes, sir." Mihran rose to his feet, but his right knee started to give. He braced himself against the handrail to keep from falling.

"If I was you, I'd go this way." The policeman pointed toward Tulare Street. "Now get the hell out of here."

Chapter Sixteen

Henry could see by the way Mihran moved that he was trying to downplay the injuries. His nephew clearly favored his left foot when he walked, and he braced himself on the arms of the chair before lowering his body into the cushion.

"Jesus, look at you." Arak tilted Mihran's head to the side and examined the bruise forming on his brother's face.

"I'll be all right in a couple of days," Mihran said.

Arak poured two generous shots of bourbon into a glass and handed it to his brother. Mihran accepted the drink with a nod of thanks.

"Just like a goddamed Turk, huh?" Arak said. "Real brave when he's in a crowd."

"How many of them were there?" Henry asked.

"Five." Mihran took a long sip of his drink. "Plus a few women standing around."

"That's probably every damned Turk in the valley," Arak said. "I just hope they show up at the next picnic."

"No, you don't," Henry said. "This is not the time to draw attention. The more distance between you and the Turks, the better."

Henry turned to Mihran. "What did you tell Teresa?"

"Nothing." Mihran winced as he adjusted his weight in the chair. "I told her I couldn't see her tonight, that you wanted to talk to me. And I'll just figure out ways to avoid her for the next few days."

"Smart," Arak said.

The conversation was cut short by a rap at the door. Arak answered it and returned with Ricky Anaforian. Anaforian was not wearing his police uniform.

Henry rose to shake policeman's hand. Mihran started to push himself up from the chair, but Anaforian signaled for him to stay where he was. Henry offered a drink, which Anaforian readily accepted. Arak poured.

Anaforian nodded toward Mihran. "You could file charges, you know. I wouldn't mind making that arrest myself."

"We're trying to avoid attention right now," Henry said. "Better to put this behind us."

"That makes sense."

Henry took his seat. Arak and Anaforian did the same.

"So what can you tell us?" Henry asked.

"I can tell you that those Turks are a stupid bunch," Anaforian said. "They thought they could just show up at the DA's office. No appointment or anything. That's what they were doing at the courthouse. They tell the gal working at the desk that they *demand* to see Robertson. Can you believe those guys? Demand?"

"Did Robertson meet with them?" Henry asked.

"Hell, no." Anaforian drained most of his bourbon in one gulp. "What did they expect? He sent them packing."

"Why did they want to meet with the DA?" Arak asked.

"That accident," Anaforian said. "They don't believe the car just ran off the road by itself. They want an investigation. At least that's what they told the receptionist."

"The police already investigated," Arak said. "I already talked to that detective Logan."

"It just shows you." Anaforian finished his drink and set the empty glass on the coffee table. Arak moved to refill it. "Those Turks don't even know the way things work in this country. They ought to go back to where they came from."

"Is the DA going to get involved?" Henry asked.

"He can't do nothing unless there's evidence of a crime," Anaforian said. "And so far, they got no evidence. So there's nothing for him to do."

"No evidence," Henry said.

"Right now, it's a one-car accident," Anaforian said. "Nothing to say otherwise. No witnesses. No physical evidence. Nothing."

"What about the two injured Turks?" Mihran asked. "What's the report on them?"

"Nothing new that I've heard."

"And what have you heard?" Mihran asked.

"They're not talking, if that's what you mean."

"I mean, what's their medical condition?"

"As far as I know, same as before," Anaforian said.

"So they're not able to talk?" Arak asked.

"Not yet, anyway," Anaforian said.

"And if they do?" Arak asked.

"Then that's another story," Anaforian said. "Depends on what they say. Might end up being one person's word against another."

Anaforian looked Mihran's way. Henry and Arak did not. Everyone took a sip of bourbon.

"Is Logan still investigating?" Henry asked.

"He hasn't closed the case," Anaforian said. "But unless something new pops up, he should pretty soon."

"Anything else you can tell us?" Henry asked.

"That's it for now." Anaforian drained the last of his drink. "I should probably get out of here."

"We appreciate your help," Henry said.

Everyone except Mihran stood.

"We know you're taking a risk talking to us," Arak said. "You're a good man."

Anaforian stared past them for a moment. He seemed to be measuring his response.

"My grandfather disappeared one night in 1915," Anaforian said. "Nobody has to thank me for anything."

Chapter Seventeen

Arak made a point of getting to the farm early. Stories about the broken window and the row of destroyed grapes would have spread rapidly, and he wanted the pickers to feel his presence. Several families waited in front of the barn for the truck that would take them to their assigned rows. Most of the workers wore long-sleeve shirts, tattered at the edges and stained by perspiration. They would suffer in the afternoon heat, but their arms would be protected.

Mothers placed a hand on their little ones to keep them quiet when Arak passed by. A few pickers nodded in his direction, but most avoided eye contact. One worker stood by himself watching the scene from afar. Arak recognized the lone picker as Enrico, the angry young man who had come to his office with Ricardo a few days earlier. Enrico leaned against a stack of empty crates with his arms crossed, striking the pose of a man who would begrudgingly fall into line with the other workers only when he had to. Arak could easily picture Enrico walking down a row of picked grapes or tossing a large piece of granite through his window.

Two of the regular farmhands drove up in the flatbed truck. Leon jumped out of the passenger seat and froze when he saw Arak.

"What are you doing here so early?" Leon asked. "Is something wrong?"

"Not so far today," Arak said louder than he needed to. "I'm just here to make sure it stays that way."

Leon nodded cautiously. He tossed several bundles of paper trays into the back of the truck and lowered the rear gate. The workers quietly climbed aboard, sitting in small groups on the stained and dusty wooden bed. Enrico took the last spot.

Arak opened the office door slowly and surveyed the room before entering. Everything was just as he had left it the night before, an observation he accepted with a trace of disappointment. If a confrontation was brewing, he would rather it came sooner than later. Each day the vandalism went unpunished was a day of shared smiles and satisfaction among the pickers. Satisfaction that came at his expense.

He was still organizing his thoughts when someone knocked on the door. Arak pushed his chair away from the desk and readied himself to rise and face whoever it was. He would not be caught off guard.

"Come in."

A woman about his age opened the door. It took Arak a few seconds to recognize her as Leon's younger sister, Nicole. He lowered his shoulders and moved to greet her.

"This is a surprise," Arak said. "What brings you out here?"

"Leon forgot his lunch," Nicole said. "I thought I could catch him before he took off, but I guess I just missed him. And then I thought, while I'm here, I should stop by and say hello."

"Have a seat." Arak gestured toward the wooden chair by the desk, but Nicole only set her purse on the desk and remained standing. She was dressed for office work in a peach blouse and a navy blue skirt. Her dark lipstick had been applied recently, possibly just before she came through the door, which highlighted the hint of red in her shoulder-length hair.

"It's been a while," Nicole said.

"Indeed."

"You go to many dances these days?"

She still had her way of making a direct reference with an indirect comment. Arak could not help but smile at the reminiscence.

"Not many. Serena's not much of a dancer."

"Too bad. You were pretty good."

They shared a knowing grin. The Fourth of July dance at the California Hotel Ballroom. Three weeks after they had graduated from high school. They'd known each other all their lives, but it wasn't until that night that he really noticed her for the first time. He happened to glance her way and was instantly captivated by the most perfect smile on the most lovely face he had ever seen. Sometime when he hadn't been paying attention, the bookworm who mostly kept to herself had become a startlingly attractive woman. Their eyes locked, and from there the mystery of mutual attraction did its work. An evening of dancing ended in a hotel room seven floors above the ballroom. For two very hot months they were inseparable, and then Nicole went away to college. But not just any college. Wellesley College, an elite school for girls on the east coast. No one he knew had ever heard of it. She promised to write, but he was not surprised that she never did. The summer had been a convenient arrangement, something they both had tacitly understood from the start. As far as he knew, she had never again set foot in Fresno until her widowed father passed away. That was two months ago. According to the stories Serena brought home, Nicole had not bothered to attend the funeral.

"I hear you're managing the business now," Nicole said. "How does it feel to be the boss?"

"A lot of work. A lot of headaches. But I like it."

"And you've got two girls."

"Ana and Eliz. Four and two. They're a handful. But they're beautiful."

"I would expect nothing less."

"How about you?"

"I'm working." She pulled a pack of Salems out of her purse. Before he could reach for a match, she had a lit cigarette between her lips. She dropped the spent match into the ash tray on his desk in a practiced motion. It was the first time he had seen her smoke.

"Three weeks now at Schilling and Marrota," Nicole said.

"The real estate guys? How's that going?"

"You happen to be talking to a real estate professional. Very important job. I do some very crucial typing. Not to mention the critical filing and mailing."

Arak waited to see if this was a topic she wanted to pursue. He gestured once more toward the empty chair, but Nicole seemed not to notice.

"I heard what happened at the picnic on Sunday," she said.

"You mean that business with the Turks?"

"I wasn't surprised."

"You knew the Turks would be there?"

"I wasn't surprised it was you who told them to leave. That sounds like the guy I used to know. It got me thinking about you again."

Nicole shifted her weight and leaned one shoulder slightly forward. It was the stance of a self-assured woman.

"In case you're about to ask," she said. "I'm not married. And I'm not romantically involved. Nor have I been. Not seriously."

"I see."

"Worried I'll end up an old maid?"

"Not at all. I'd say a woman like you can afford to be choosy."

"Choosy." She smiled as if the word reminded her of a joke. "Choosy is good, I suppose. Unless the pickings are slim."

"Pickings any better on the east coast?"

"Leaving this town was the best decision I ever made," she said. "One of only two things I did while I was living here that I'm proud of. It really pissed my father off. But I was eighteen, and I had a scholarship. There wasn't a damned thing he could do about it."

"I was sorry to hear about your father."

"Leon's the one I worry about."

"It's good that you're here for him."

"Of course, it is." She took a long draw on her cigarette.

"So what was the other thing?" Arak asked. "What else made you proud of yourself?"

"You." She said this as if the answer were obvious. "Our summer."

He could only nod at her characteristic bluntness.

"I learned a lot about myself," she said. "And then I left."

"And now you're back."

"I am." A barely perceptible look of sadness crossed her face. "For now."

"Home is always home."

"I sure as hell hope not."

"You don't feel a connection?"

"To what?"

"To your family?"

"It's just me and Leon."

"To Armenian Town?"

Nicole let out a laugh and flicked ashes off the tip of her cigarette into the ash tray. It was a motion by someone who had been smoking for a long time.

"Armenian Town is breaking up, Arak. Actually, more like dissolving. Or haven't you noticed?"

"A few people have moved away."

"Lots of people," she said. "It's just the old generation that won't let go. Most of the kids don't give a rat's ass about the whole community thing. To them, it's history."

"They're still Armenians."

"They've still got an *i-a-n* at the end of their name, if that's what you mean. And even that's going away. Look at how many are marrying outside the tribe. Like your brother. Or so I hear."

"There's always been a lot of that."

"Another thirty years and Armenians will be just another ethnic group that once migrated *en masse* to this part of the country. When you tell someone you're an Armenian, you'll have to explain what that means."

"I can't tell if that makes you happy or sad."

"I was one of the first to leave, remember?"

"But you came back."

She put out her cigarette in the ashtray. "Someone has to look after Leon."

Arak was suddenly aware of her perfume, a flowery scent that had been lingering under the wisps of cigarette smoke. The fragrance seemed out-of-place this early in the day.

"How about we change the topic?" she said.

"Sure."

"What time do you get off work?"

"Hard to say. Five. Maybe six. It's a busy time of the year."

"I could come by later." Nicole took one step forward and dipped one shoulder. The peach blouse billowed slightly open, revealing the edge of her white bra. She extended her smallest finger and lightly stroked the side of his neck. It was a gesture she had used years earlier to signal her mood.

"What are you doing?" he asked.

"Getting nostalgic." She placed her hands on his shoulders and then slid her palms around the back of his neck.

Arak put his hands on her hips. He paused for a second before pushing her away.

"What the hell?" she said.

"No."

"No what?"

"I'm sorry."

"No spark?"

"It's not that."

"I'm a big girl. You don't have to protect my feelings."

"I'm married."

"I'm not interested in breaking up your family."

"What then? Just sex?"

"Would it be so bad?" She grabbed the end of his belt and tugged. The buckle unfastened.

Arak took a step back and quietly re-fastened his belt.

"Oh God," she said. "Don't tell me. You've got principles. A set of high standards that give your life meaning."

"What's wrong with principles?"

"Nothing." Nicole threw her arms in the air. "My father had principles. He always knew what was right for everyone."

She lit a second cigarette, waved the match out and tossed it toward the ash tray but missed.

"The men I work for have principles," she said. "When they're not trying to get around the law or trying to screw someone out of their money. Or when they're not busy patting me on the ass with their grimy little hands."

"I can only speak for myself," Arak said. "Some things are very important to me. My family. My children. My people. And I'll fight for what I believe in."

"It must be very reassuring to have all the answers."

"I never said I had all the answers."

"Maybe I should find myself some of these principles. That would solve everything, wouldn't it? Where do you find them, at Holy Trinity? Is Father Hoogasian still there? Is he still telling the girls that if they work real hard maybe they can catch a wonderful Armenian husband and have his children?"

"I get that things aren't so great for you right now," he said.

"Don't." She held up an open palm. "You have no idea."

Nicole sat on the wooden chair in front of Arak's desk, set her cigarette on the edge of the ash tray, and stared at the smoke curling into the air. She seemed suddenly much smaller; her confidence had disappeared. She looked like a defeated boxer slumped on a stool.

"I'd like it if you would come around once in a while," he said.

"Sure. Why not?"

"Maybe after things settle down around here. After picking season."

"When's that? A couple of weeks from now? I don't plan that far ahead."

"You thinking of leaving again?"

She picked up her cigarette and brought it toward her lips. "I dream of leaving again."

Chapter Eighteen

Teresa sat on the floor clutching her knees and waiting for the last wave to pass. Objects in the room slowly came back into focus. She lifted her weak arms above her head as a way to reassure herself that her strength was returning. Her heart was still pounding, but her breathing was slowing. Soon she would be all right.

It had been three months since her last panic attack, the longest gap ever. She had even begun to entertain the possibility that they were a thing of the past, a hope now dashed. Countless high school afternoons in the library had made her an expert on the topic. Not that knowledge seemed to help. On one point, she and the experts disagreed. The attacks were supposed to come out of nowhere, triggered by an unconscious association. But, at least in this most recent case, she was fully aware of the source.

She was the one who had raised the topic. She had peppered Mihran with questions early in their relationship. Yes, he said, Armenians are Christians. The Saropians belong to the Holy Trinity Apostolic Church. Did he attend? Occasionally. To be with the family? More to be part of the community. Did he believe? Still an open question.

Then it was her turn. Of course, her family was Catholic. Ever know an Irish family that wasn't? No, she didn't attend. Not since she was thirteen. Believe? Don't even ask.

She had dutifully participated in all the Saropian rituals except one. But Mihran was persistent, and she had run out of excuses. And so, as promised, this coming Sunday she would join Mihran and his family for church services. At the time, she really thought she could do it. Maybe she still could.

Teresa stretched out on the carpet, closed her eyes, and allowed

herself to recall her own childhood church. St. Anthony's was over-
whelming to a little girl. She was intimidated by the radiant stained
glass figures who looked down on her from either side. The reverberating organ sent chills up and down her spine, as if God himself were
making his presence known. And in the middle of it all was Father
Hennessey. Standing above the gathering in his swaying black robe,
his words resonating over their heads and echoing off the towering
walls and cavernous ceiling. The voice that would rise and fall with
messages the girl did not fully understand, but delivered in a tone
that spoke of something special, something more powerful and more
important than she was capable of achieving alone. Surely Father
Hennessey was the link to God. When she did something she wasn't
supposed to, it was not God she feared might be watching. It was
Father Hennessey, passing judgment on the imperfect girl who knew
right but sometimes did wrong.

She had been the best Catholic girl of them all. Prayers every
night. Mass every Sunday. Perfect Catechism attendance. Helping
with the youth program as soon as she turned 12. And doing volun-
teer work in the church office after school three days a week. The first
time Father Hennessey entered the office and she found herself only
a few feet from the man, her muscles seemed to leave her. Her breath
came in small gasps, and she had to brace herself against the counter
to keep from falling. Later, when he asked her name, the words that
came out of her mouth were so soft that he feigned a hearing diffi-
culty and apologized for asking her to repeat. Father was no more
than average height at best, and as a tall thirteen-year-old, she was
but a few inches shorter. Yet when he looked down at her, the difference seemed immense.

Even as the incident unfolded that afternoon, she could not fully
process what was happening. Her knowledge of such matters was
limited to one vague paragraph and a couple of line drawings in a
pamphlet one of the girls had passed around earlier that year. Whatever ideas she had about sex were filtered through naive romantic
themes she had picked up from movies and books. And so, when
Father stroked her hair and put his hands on her blouse, the experience was so removed from anything she had ever imagined that she
doubted her senses. Things simply could not be what they seemed.

It was only later that night as she lay awake in her own room
that she could begin to put the scattered images into a sequence. His

rough whiskers against her cheek. Lifting her skirt and pulling down her underwear. Her face pressed against the hard wood floor. And the hum of street traffic just on the other side of the window curtains. And even then, there were moments she could reproduce only by looking at them from afar, as if she were a spectator watching from the other side of a protective pane of glass.

The next morning, she claimed to have an upset stomach and spent the day hidden under blankets in a darkened room. She sank into what she would later understand to be an episode of depression that lasted for months.

She once tried to tell her mother. A week, maybe two, after the day. But before she could finish the story, her mother slapped her across the face.

"You filthy child," her mother screamed. "You lying, filthy child. Never, ever repeat your blasphemous lies to anyone. Have you no respect for what is holy?"

Her mother slapped her again. The conversation was over. It was the only time her mother ever struck her.

Teresa stopped going to church, and her mother never asked why. She developed strategies to blunt her emotions and in time came to think of herself as resilient and self-reliant. But the price was isolation and loneliness. Throughout high school she avoided social events where boys and girls mingled. Dating was out of the question. Even friendships with other girls were kept on the other side of a line that required a trust she could not generate.

Her only promise of relief came from the thought of going away to college someday. When that time finally arrived, her mother's objections were half-hearted at best. There were closer and better schools. But Teresa insisted, and that was that. As always, her father watched everything from a distance. Moving away reduced but did not eliminate the panic attacks, and she was left with the passage of time as her only source of healing.

And then she met Mihran. There were the surface sources of attraction. The quick smile and the clever insights. But she also perceived a seriousness just under the surface that set him apart. He answered her questions. He acknowledged his weaknesses. And she found herself confiding in him. Small things, but the first acts of trust she had attempted in years. She sensed that Mihran also held secrets yet to be revealed, something that gave him a seductive air of intrigue. Most important, she perceived an implied promise that he would always be there for her. More than anything, he gave her hope.

Teresa opened her eyes and sat up. She had fallen asleep. The breeze pushing its way through the open window chilled her perspiration-soaked blouse and carried into the room the smoky vapors of a nearby barbeque. It was nearly dark. She rearranged her weight on the thin carpet and listened to the sounds of the evening. She heard the clatter of kitchenware as the couple next door prepared dinner, bits of a conversation between people gathered somewhere near the street, and June Christy's silky voice rising from a neighbor's record player. There was a rhythm and a melody to the moment that gave her a vague sense of attachment with her neighbors as well as a keen awareness that she was living on her own.

Chapter Nineteen

The farmhands were done for the day. The equipment was stowed, picked and unpicked rows of grapes had been counted. Trays and frames and crates were stacked and ready for the morning. The pickers had retreated to their temporary homes where they would prepare their meals and later sit outside with other families to share food and drink and the camaraderie that develops among strangers in common circumstances. Only Arak remained on the job, tending to the details that came with the frenzy of the season. The entire year's efforts depended on getting the grapes picked, dried, rolled and shipped on time while under the ever-present threat of an early crop-damaging rain. It was Arak's first time managing the entire process on his own. In a way, a test of his ability to handle the job. Which was why he wasn't surprised when Henry stopped by to see how things were going. How many acres left to pick? Did he have enough cash on hand? How were they doing on trays? Arak calmly answered each question. So far, he was passing the test.

He and Henry stood in front of the office in the shadows cast by the last of the day's punishing sun. His uncle was dispensing what Arak hoped were his last few pieces of advice when they heard the rapid pounding of approaching footsteps. They looked up to find Leon and Kenny running toward them.

"Arak! Arak!" Leon cried. He and Kenny came to an abrupt halt several yards away when they saw Henry.

"Mr. Saropian," Leon said between gasps of air.

"Mr. Saropian," Kenny repeated.

"Good evening, men," Henry said.

The farmhands took the greeting as an invitation to approach.

"What's the problem?" Arak asked.

111

"We was down by the tool shed," Leon said. "And we saw these Mexicans coming out the door. And they had some things in their arms. Some shovels and hand saws. That's what they looked like to me."

Leon turned to Kenny for confirmation. Kenny, an angular young man with a protruding chin and narrow eyes, picked up the story.

"We hid over by the plum trees and just watched," Kenny said. "Then those Mexicans — there was three of them — they grabbed a couple of the empty crates that was stacked up there. And they took them and the shovels and the other stuff and went off."

"How did they get into the shed?" Arak asked.

The two farmhands looked at one another.

"The door might not have been locked." Kenny glanced at Henry for a reaction then quickly looked away.

"Did you see where they went?" Arak asked.

"No, sir," Kenny said. "We came right here to find you."

"Did you bother to notice what direction they were headed?" Arak asked. "Was it out toward the pond where they burned the crates last time?"

"Yes, sir." Leon was so excited that he was bouncing from foot to foot. "That's just the direction they was headed."

"You boys stay here." Arak and Henry walked toward the Cadillac. The farmhands dutifully remained where they were.

"We've got to put an end to this," Arak said. "They're not going to stop until we do something."

"I suppose you're right," Henry said.

"If these guys get away with it, what's to prevent the others?"

"It's only a few trouble-makers."

"Right now, it's only a few."

"But we can't put up with this destruction."

"Now's our chance," Arak said. "We know where they are."

"I have to be going." Henry opened the door to his car but did not get inside. He glanced at the two farmhands who watched eagerly from a distance.

"They're rubbing it in our face," Arak said. "We can't just take it."

"You're right," Henry said. "Do what you have to."

"I'll give you a full report in the morning."

"Don't bother." Henry slid into the car. "I'd rather not hear the details."

Chapter Twenty

The sun had set by the time Mihran left the office. Work had piled up all week, in large part because of the distractions he had carried into the office each day. Jack had taken a long look when Mihran limped through the door that morning. The knee had stiffened during the night. But Jack, a private man himself, rarely asked people about their lives outside of work, and this morning was no exception. Several cups of coffee had allowed Mihran to fend off the exhaustion that threatened to overtake him all day. By the time he flicked off the lights and locked the door, he appeared to be the only person in the twelve-story building besides the janitors.

Aspirin was his only defense against the throbbing in his swollen knee, and the walk home was more painful than the walk coming in. He was within half a block of his house when Mihran heard someone call to him.

"Mihran. Hey, Mihran."

He spun in the direction of the voice. His arms were raised, ready to defend himself.

"Easy, champ." A uniformed policeman stepped out of the shadow of a large oak tree. It was Anaforian. "I been waiting for you."

Mihran dropped his arms. "Sorry."

"After what happened to you yesterday, I'd be a little jumpy my-self."

"You want to come inside?" Mihran gestured toward the house.

"No thanks." Anaforian looked quickly in both directions. "We can talk out here."

"Is this about what happened on Sunday?"

Anaforian nodded, as if to signal that the fewer words exchanged the better.

"You want me to get Arak and my uncle?" Mihran asked in a lowered voice.

"You're the one I need to talk to."

Mihran waited.

"Arak told Logan that you and him drove home from the picnic," Anaforian said. "He said you didn't see the Turks or the accident."

"That's right."

"And Arak said you stopped at Vincent's Grocery on the way home."

"That's right, too."

"Said you didn't see anyone except Vincent there."

Mihran nodded.

"Not even coming or going," Anaforian said.

"What are you getting at?"

The policeman shuffled his feet and glanced around once more. "Vincent says different."

"What does Vincent say?" Mihran asked.

"He says you and Arak arrived the same time the Turks were leaving."

"Did Vincent say we were in the store the same time as the Turks?"

"He didn't say that," Anaforian said. "But he thinks you might have run into the Turks outside the store. When they were leaving and you were arriving."

"How can he know that?"

"Vincent said Arak was talking about the Turks when he paid for his cigarettes. And that Arak told him he shouldn't let Turks shop there just because they got money."

"Is that a problem?" Mihran asked.

"Vincent's version of events don't quite square with Arak's," Anaforian said. "And that's a problem for Logan."

"How big a problem?"

"Could be real big."

Anaforian glanced around once more.

"I'm the only one in the department who really understands this thing," Anaforian said. "That Logan. He don't know the difference between an Armenian and a Turk. Calls both of them Fresno Indians. Says it right in front of me, the bastard. But he's the detective on this one. And it makes him suspicious that Arak might be lying about seeing the Turks at the grocery store."

"Why are you telling me this?" Mihran asked.

"Logan's going to want to talk with you," Anaforian said. "This thing could come down to who Logan wants to believe. And it would help a lot if you and Arak were saying the same thing."

"Got it."

"I heard something else you might be interested in," Anaforian said. "That scuffle you got into yesterday at the courthouse?"

"More like I was attacked."

"There's one guy who's causing all the trouble," Anaforian said. "His name is Aybar. Deniz Aybar. Tall guy. Pretty strong, too. You know which guy I'm talking about?"

"I remember him." Having a name to go with the face somehow made the man more threatening.

"This Aybar's the one that decided they should talk to the D.A.," Anaforian said. "After the D.A. wouldn't see him, they went to the newspaper. Aybar told some reporter that the police and the D.A. won't do anything about the accident."

"How do you know what he told the reporter?"

"The reporter calls the police station," Anaforian said. "They talk to Logan. Logan talks to me."

"Is there going to be something in the paper?"

"My guess is yes. And this is the kind of thing that drives people crazy. The last thing anyone wants is bad publicity. The sooner this whole thing is resolved, the better."

"So what's this Deniz Aybar's story?"

"The guy hurt in the accident," Anaforian said. "The one driving the car. Emin Aybar. That's his brother."

Mihran nodded. The newspaper photographs of Emin and Hazan Aybar returned to him.

"He's the one you got to look out for," Anaforian said. "I thought you should know."

Before Mihran could respond, Fresno's only Armenian police officer turned his back and walked away. The conversation was over.

Chapter Twenty-One

The flames were several feet high when Arak and the two farm-hands reached the irrigation pond. An orange reflection splashed across the still surface of the water. The dry wood crackled. Arak positioned himself behind a row of grapevines and motioned for Leon and Kenny to do the same. Only a thin line on the horizon remained from the day's light.

"Same place as before," Leon whispered.

"Where we can easily find the remains," Arak said.

"That don't make no sense."

"It does if you want the owner to know what you've done."

Three migrant workers stood facing the fire, their bodies dark silhouettes against the glow. Each held what appeared to be a bottle of beer in his hand. The shortest of the three grabbed a shovel by the wooden handle and tossed it into the flames. The other two cheered. The short man turned toward his companions, revealing his profile.

"Enrico," Arak said softly.

Enrico tossed the remains of a wooden crate into the fire, and then all three pickers sat in the soft soil with their backs to the vineyard.

"They're going to hang around and enjoy themselves," Arak said. "Looks like one more shovel to go. When it's gone, we make our move."

Several minutes passed before one of the migrants rose to fling his empty bottle toward the pond. The bottle disappeared into the dark sky. A splash followed. The man staggered a little as he grabbed the remaining shovel and hurled it into the fire. Arak made note of the underdeveloped body outlined against the flames. The body of a teenager. The unsteady walk suggested that the boy had been drinking for a while.

Arak turned toward Leon and Kenny. In the dim light provided by the fire, he raised the wooden wheelbarrow handle he had taken from the barn. The two farmhands lifted their own makeshift weapons, a handle from a short hoe and a three-foot 2 by 4. It was time to move.

Drunken Spanish banter and the crackling of the fire allowed them to move to within a few feet of their targets without notice. Then Leon stumbled over a clump of dry weeds. Enrico turned in time to see Arak's wheelbarrow handle coming down on him. The worker threw an arm up in time to catch the thickest part of the club across his forearm. The blow landed with a crack. Enrico leaned forward clutching his arm. Arak snapped the man's head back with a heel to the chin. In a desperate attempt to protect himself, Enrico held his good arm in front of his face with fingers spread wide. Arak snapped the wooden handle across the top of the fingers. Enrico screamed and fell backward onto the soil.

Arak moved to assist the others. Leon was smacking the teenager across the back with the 2 by 4 as the boy tried to crawl away. Arak placed the heel of his boot under the worker's side and rolled him onto his back. The boy pulled his legs up to protect himself and held his hands in front of his face. Arak instructed Leon to keep hitting.

Kenny's man had rolled himself into a ball and had covered his head with his hands. Arak kicked him in the side. When the migrant placed an open palm against the ground to right himself, Arak brought the heel of his boot down in the middle of the hand. He beat the man's fingers with the wheelbarrow handle until both hands were bloody.

Then Arak returned to Enrico. The small man tried to push himself off the ground, but his arm gave way. He fell face first into the soil and stayed there. Arak stood over him.

"You're not picking any more grapes this year," Arak said. "Not with those hands. And if I find you or your two buddies anywhere near this farm, I'm hauling your ass off to the police. You can spend the rest of this and the next picking season in jail."

Enrico made no movement and said nothing.

Arak leaned forward. "Just who the hell did you think you were dealing with?"

Chapter Twenty-Two

Teresa closed the apartment door behind her and dropped into her one good chair, the olive green mismatch given to her by the girls who moved out of the apartment next door. She set the mail and the afternoon paper on the floor, closed her eyes, and listened to the throb of the headache she had been nursing all day. It was back-to-school time, and she had been on her feet helping surly mothers and uncooperative children pick out new clothes since 9:00 that morning. If Teresa ever needed motivation to stay in school, she had only to look at the "lifers" — the men and women who supported themselves and sometimes a family working full-time at Gottschalk's. They complained about the job more than anyone, but they were the first to sign up for the extra weekend shift. Teresa never asked why they didn't just quit. The answer was obvious.

She found the newspaper and scanned the headlines, making a point to avoid the ads for women's apparel. She didn't have the energy to admire what she couldn't afford. She was moving quickly through the second section, thinking as much about dinner as the words she was reading, when a headline caught her eye:

Turkish Students Demand Accident Investigation

She read the story twice then glanced at her watch. Mihran would still be at work. She picked up the phone and dialed.

"Have you seen the afternoon paper?" Teresa asked.

"Not yet," Mihran said. "I'm here for at least another hour."

"There's a story you need to read."

"What about?"

"There was an accident on Clovis Avenue Sunday. Two Turkish students from the college were hurt pretty badly. Some other students think it was no accident. They went to the newspaper. They want an investigation."

"I'll have to read that when I get home." He seemed to be choosing his words carefully.

"The students say they were threatened at a confrontation earlier in the day," she said. "At a picnic in Kingsburg."

"What are you getting at?"

"That's got to be the Armenian picnic. The one we were at."

"I suppose so."

"They said one of the picnic organizers told them to leave and then threatened them. Mihran, the person they're talking about has to be Arak."

"The police have already looked into it. Trust me, it's nothing to worry about."

"You know about this?"

"Really, it's nothing."

"Did Arak threaten to hurt those students?"

"Arak told them to leave. That's all."

"Mihran, you rode home with Arak. Do the police know that?"

"They know."

"So you've talked with them?"

"Arak talked with them."

"Why don't I know anything about this?"

"Because there's nothing to know."

"It's in the newspaper," Teresa said. "How could you keep this from me?"

"We're dealing with it," Mihran said. "Until the damned Turks went to the paper, it was all being handled quietly."

"Being handled," she said. "Does *being handled* mean not even telling your fiancé?"

"Please don't make more out of this than it is."

"What does it take, Mihran? Do we have to be married before you treat me like a member of the family?"

"That's got nothing to do with it," he said. "Serena doesn't know. At least she didn't until today. And neither did my mother."

"So it's just for the men to deal with?"

"Something like that, yes."

Teresa considered whether to pursue the point or take the conversation in a different direction.

"The students Arak told to leave," she said. "Do they know it was Arak? Do they know his name?"

"Not according to the police."

"And how do you know that?"

"I know."

"What if they find out?" she asked. "They're angry about the accident. Who knows what they might do?"

"They're not going to find out."

"There were a lot of people at the picnic. I don't know how you keep a lid on something like that."

"We're talking about Armenians and Turks," Mihran said. "Believe me, no Armenian is going to say anything to help any Turk."

"What if the police talk with you?"

"What if they do?"

"What if they ask you what happened after the picnic?"

"Then I'll tell them."

"Tell them the truth?"

"I told you before, there's nothing to worry about."

"So we're back to that."

They both endured a long silence.

"This is not the right way to have this discussion," he said. "Can I come by tonight? Buy you dinner?"

"I don't think so," she said. "Not tonight. I've had a long day."

"Tomorrow?"

"We'll see."

Chapter Twenty-Three

Henry stared at the amber ring of liquid at the bottom of his glass. He made his way to the liquor cabinet where he found the Jack Daniel's and poured a refill. He could not remember the last time he had consumed liquor when alone. The second drink went down more smoothly than the first. The third he barely noticed.

Arak arrived a few minutes after 8:00. Henry set his empty glass in the kitchen sink before answering the door. He could feel the alcohol and was mindful of his movements and speech as he invited his nephew into the den. He offered Arak a drink, then poured one for himself in a new glass. They sat across from one another, Arak on the couch and Henry in his usual place in the large recliner.

"Can you believe the newspaper printing that crap?" Arak said. "Since when do Turks have a say in what gets into the paper?"

Henry responded by taking a sip of his drink.

"Where's that little brother of mine?" Arak glanced at his watch.

"Mihran's not coming," Henry said.

Arak set his drink aside and leaned forward. "So what's this about?"

"One of our pickers came to see me this morning."

"Which one?"

"Which one is not important." Henry took a deep breath. "He told me about last night. About the three workers. The ones we heard were stealing shovels and crates."

"And?"

"You tell me. What happened?"

"What did you hear?"

"Just tell me what happened."

"We found the guys," Arak said. "They were out by the pond burning the stuff they stole, just like before. And they were drunk. Me and Leon and Kenny hit them a few times. We had some boards and tool handles. That sort of thing. We taught them a lesson. And I made sure they knew who we were and why we had come after them."

"I heard you broke their fingers." Henry was surprised to see that his glass was almost empty again. "And one man's wrist. Is that true?"

"Could be. They held their hands up to protect themselves."

"Was that your intention?"

"We did what we set out to do."

"But broken fingers?" Henry said. "A broken wrist?"

"It happens." Arak shrugged.

"Some of the workers have families to provide for. If they can't pick, they can't live."

"Maybe they should have thought of that before they decided to destroy someone else's property."

"They burnt some crates," Henry said. "A few shovels. The punishment hardly fits the crime."

"They were sending a message. Putting it right in our faces. It had to stop."

"Not that way, it didn't."

"So what are you saying?" Arak found his glass and took a long drink before continuing. "Are you saying that you didn't know what was going to happen?"

"I didn't know. Not that. I didn't think you'd leave them in that condition."

"Then what? You thought we were just going to give them a good talking to?"

"I thought you'd threaten them," Henry said. "Maybe rough them up a little. But not maim them."

Arak stepped to the liquor cabinet and poured himself a second drink.

"You knew," Arak said, his back still turned away from Henry.

"I didn't."

"You could have stopped me." Arak spun toward his uncle. "But you chose not to."

"Are you calling me a liar?"

"You said you didn't want to hear the details. But why would the details matter if we were just going to scare them?"

"I had no idea it would turn out this way."

"If you didn't know, it's because you didn't want to."

"Don't you challenge me," Henry said. "I said I didn't know."

"I heard you." Arak returned to the couch. "But tell me, who are you trying to convince?"

Henry waited before responding. Unlike his nephew, he understood the danger of acting or speaking impulsively.

"I want you to find Roberto," Henry said. "First thing tomorrow morning. Tell him I need to talk to him."

"Roberto wasn't one of them."

"The three men you beat up are gone," Henry said. "But Roberto will probably know where they went. I'm not quite sure how yet, but we need to make this thing right."

"You're bringing those thieves back to the farm?"

"I don't see that as the solution," Henry said. "But maybe we can take care of their doctor bills. I don't know. Make sure they get by until they can work again."

"Are you kidding me?"

"We need to do something."

"I don't believe this."

"*I* need to do something."

"Can you imagine how that will make me look?" Arak asked. "Every Mexican in the valley will hear about it. How will I ever be able to control those people?"

"Is that what this is about?" Henry asked. "Controlling people?"

"When pickers destroy our property, you're damned right I need to control that."

"There are better ways."

"Somebody has to pay," Arak said. "You can't just let them get away with it."

"Nobody got away with anything," Henry said. "The workers all know what happened."

"Are you afraid they'll retaliate?" Arak said. "I wouldn't worry about it. Not after what happened to those three. Not unless they want the same. Or worse."

"Don't you ever learn?"

"They're the ones who destroyed our property."

"It's not as simple as that."

"You think paying them off will stop it?" Arak said. "You think that's good business?"

"It's not about business."

"Then what?"

"Never mind." Henry rose to get another drink. "Just get out of here."

"You still want me to find Roberto in the morning?"

"Just leave. I'll figure this out on my own."

Chapter Twenty-Four

Mihran watched from the couch as Teresa prepared gin and tonics in the kitchen. They had avoided the inevitable discussion to this point, observing an implicit agreement to keep their meal as pleasant as possible. He had taken her to the Cathay Inn on Van Ness and insisted that she do all the ordering. Chow mein, sliced pork, and even the deep-fried battered shrimp that he had yet to develop a taste for. Although his knee still ached, he was determined to hide the limp he had struggled with the past two days. As far as he could tell, Teresa had not noticed any difference in his step.

She turned on the radio, turned down the lights, and set the drinks on the table in front of him. Nat King Cole's velvety voice filled the room.

"I think it's time you told me what's going on." Teresa sat on the opposite end of the couch and curled her legs up underneath her so that she could face him. "You know. The Turks. The accident. Arak. You."

"Sometimes people are better off not knowing things." Mihran took a long sip of his drink. "And I honestly think this is one of those times."

"Does Serena know the whole story?" she asked.

"I'm sure she does not."

"Then it's just who? You, Arak and your Uncle Henry?"

"That's right. And they expect me to keep it that way."

"So it's a matter of trust."

"In a way," he said. "And you need to trust me that I'll deal with things appropriately. I wouldn't keep anything from you that you needed to know."

"Trust works both ways," she said. "How much do you trust the woman you plan to marry? Enough to share everything with her? For better or worse? 'Til death do us part?"

"Can you accept that I'm looking out for you? That the decisions I make have your best interest at heart?"

"I want to believe that."

"You *want* to?"

"Trust isn't so easy for me." Her voice was suddenly softer.

"And why is that?"

"Sometimes the people you believe in let you down." She folded her arms across her chest. Her eyes were distant and sad. "But I still need it. Maybe that's why I need it. Maybe even more than most people. I don't want to always wonder if I'm getting the full story from you or just a convenient part of it."

For the first time since he had known her, Teresa suddenly seemed small and alone. A child curled up on the end of the couch in need of a warm lap and reassurance.

"OK," Mihran said.

"OK what? You'll tell me?"

"I will." He set his gin and tonic on the table. "But remember trust goes both ways. I need you to keep this just between the two of us."

"Agreed." She took a deep breath. "Thank you."

And then he told her. About the encounter at Vincent's grocery. About the accident on Clovis Avenue. About the discussion between the three Saropian men that followed.

Teresa was silent for a long while before responding.

"That poor couple," she said. "This is so horrible."

"Beyond horrible."

"I don't understand your brother."

"Arak didn't mean to hurt anyone."

"Of course, he did," she said. "Maybe not the way it turned out. But don't say he's not to blame."

"Absolutely he's to blame."

"And what about you? Why didn't you stop him?"

"You're going to blame me?"

"You were there. You saw what Arak was doing."

"I pleaded with him to stop."

"What about the steering wheel? Couldn't you have grabbed it?"

"That would have been crazy. I might have killed everyone."

"You could have reached the gear shift. Thrown the car into neutral. Or into reverse."

Mihran calmed himself before answering. "I did everything I could think of at the time to stop him. You'll just have to believe me on that."

"I'm sorry," Teresa said. "It's just very upsetting. You said you talked with the police?"

"Arak has."

"And what did he say?"

"He denied knowing anything about the accident."

"And what about you?"

"I haven't talked to them yet," he said. "But I expect to soon."

"And what will you say?"

"What *can* I say? I'll back up Arak's story. If the only two witnesses agree on what happened, there's not much the police can do about it."

"So you're going to lie?"

"I'm going to support my brother."

"What if they have evidence you don't know about?" Teresa asked. "What if they have a witness?"

"There's no witness."

"You don't know that."

"I do know what would happen to Arak if I tell the police everything," Mihran said.

"You're putting yourself at risk for your brother's sake."

"I'm aware of that."

"What if there's a trial?" she asked. "What if you lie under oath? That's perjury. And then there's leaving the scene of an accident."

"I'm aware of the risks."

"What about the Turks? What if they die?"

"I hope that doesn't happen."

"And if it does? Will you still protect your brother?"

"Would putting Arak in prison bring them back?"

"Listen to you," she said. "You're always talking about justice. Justice for the innocent. Justice for all the Armenians slaughtered during the atrocities."

"Don't even begin to compare that situation with this one," he said. "There's no comparison. None."

"Why? Because they're Turks and you're Armenian?"

This time Mihran could not suppress the wave of anger that overtook him.

"Nobody slaughtered innocent women and children last Sunday." His angry voice filled the small apartment. "No one was tossed in a river or left to die in the desert. Words were exchanged. Things got out of hand. Way out of hand. I wish it had never happened. But it did."

"Two people might die." Teresa picked up their glasses. "I guess that qualifies as getting out of hand."

She disappeared into the kitchen. Mihran sat quietly and listened to his words played back in his mind. It was the first time he has raised his voice to Teresa. Several minutes passed. He knew she was standing in front of the sink thinking, like he was, about what just happened.

"I'm sorry." Teresa's soft voice wafted from the kitchen. She returned empty handed and settled back onto the couch. "The whole story just kind of caught me off guard."

"I'm sorry too," Mihran said. "It's been a difficult time."

"How long does this go on?"

"I don't know," he said. "Not much longer. A week. Maybe more."

"That's not what I meant."

"What then?"

"Are you going to teach our children to hate Turkish children?"

It was a question too important to answer right away. As Mihran considered his response, he slowly became aware of other people in the room. There was an old man dressed in a billowing *arkhaluk*. He was stooping forward and had deep folds in his dark, leathery skin. Then the outline of a boy emerged. He carried a cloth sack over his shoulder. Then a young woman in a stained blue dress holding a small child in her arms. The visitors seemed to be watching him with great patience, as if they had all the time in the world.

"Hate is not a solution," Mihran said. "But neither is forgetting."

Chapter Twenty-Five

The banging on the front door thundered through the house.

"My Lord." Tarvez stepped into the living room holding the towel she had been using to dry the breakfast dishes.

"I'll get it, Mom," Mihran said.

He waited for his mother to return to the kitchen before moving to the side of the door and glancing through the front window. How hard would it be for the Turks to learn his name? And from there, a phone book or maybe just a few questions to the right people could lead them directly to this address. Through the narrow slit Mihran could see a man's dark pant legs. From what he could tell, the man was alone.

The pounding started again. Mihran opened the door with caution.

Anaforian, in uniform, barged into the room. "We got to talk."

Mihran gestured Anaforian back onto the porch and closed the door behind them.

"The Turks are dead," Anaforian said. "Happened early this morning. First the man, then his wife. About two hours apart."

Mihran stood in place for several seconds while he struggled to process the message. The defenses he had constructed to keep this moment at bay came crashing down. He was adrift in an empty emotional space, at a loss for what to think or how to feel.

"Both of them, just this morning," Anaforian said. "Gone."

"Now what?" Mihran's mouth was dry, his voice unsteady.

"Shit's gonna fly," Anaforian said. "After what happened to you the other day. And the damned Turks already talking to the newspaper. Where's Arak?"

The question helped Mihran focus. "Probably at the farm. You know, picking season."

"You better go tell him. Henry, too."

"What happens now with the police?"

"I'm meeting Logan in half an hour," Anaforian said. "He's got to move fast. You know it will be in the *Bee* this afternoon. Shit's gonna fly. You can bet your ass on that. Shit's gonna fly."

"What else?" Mihran asked. "Tell me what else I can do."

Anaforian pointed a finger that stopped just short of Mihran's chest. "Your testimony just got a lot more important. If I was you, I'd give that a lot of thought. I'd make sure I knew exactly what I wanted to say, and then I'd stick with it."

***

Arak spent the morning working with Leon and two young farm-hands loading rolls of dried grapes into crates and onto the truck bed. He had always made a point of working with the farmhands. Pitching in not only assured that the job would be done correctly, it sent a message. Arak knew what hard work was, and he wasn't above getting his hands dirty. The payoff was respect from the farmhands and their support and loyalty when he needed it.

Hirasuna had been the only farmer in the area with enough extra crates to replace the ones burned by the migrants. The old Jap knew he had Arak over a barrel and had insisted on thirty bucks for their use. The crates were filthy and splintering, probably ones Hirasuna had already replaced but hadn't gotten around to burning himself.

When the last crate was loaded and the other farmhands moved on to their next chore, Leon stayed behind. He straightened a stack of frames, arranged and then rearranged some hand tools leaning up against the barn. Arak understood that Leon had something he wanted to say. He pretended to busy himself with something on the truck while he waited.

"Can I ask you a question?" Leon said after a few minutes had passed.

"Anything you want."

"Them guys the other night. The Mexicans down at the pond. Do you know what happened to them?"

"You saw," Arak said. "They got what they deserved. Don't you think?"

"They sure did. But after we left. What then?"

"They're gone, Leon." Arak lifted and secured the tail gate. "Probably moved up north to start picking apples."

"I heard they broke some bones."

"I don't know about that," Arak said. "But they sure learned a lesson."

"Right." Leon shifted his weight back and forth from one foot to the other. "They learned a lesson."

The conversation ended abruptly when Mihran drove up and bolted from the car.

"You weren't at home or in your office," Mihran said. "I tried calling."

"Some of us work outside," Arak said. "Even on a Saturday."

"We have to talk," Mihran said. "Alone."

Arak signaled for Leon to stay where he was. He put a hand on his brother's back and directed him back toward the car.

"What's this all about?" Arak asked.

"The Turks, Arak. The man and the woman in the accident. They died."

"When?"

"This morning. Anaforian told me."

"Did they ever recover? Did they say anything to the cops?"

"That's not the point," Mihran said. "Damn it, Arak. They're dead."

"I heard you," Arak said. "What do you expect me to say? I'm sorry? I am, you know. Sorry this happened. For whatever that's worth."

"This changes things," Mihran said. "I didn't think it would, but it does."

"It changes nothing."

"It's more serious now."

"Why?" Arak said. "Because a couple of Turks are dead? Seems to me that makes things a lot easier."

"Now we're talking about murder."

"Who's talking about murder? No one said anything about a murder."

"The Turks did. That's exactly what they told the newspaper."

"Let them," Arak said. "You heard Anaforian. A single-car accident. That's not murder."

"We've got to find Henry."

"I'll tell Henry when I see him."

"We've got to talk about this," Mihran said. "We've got to figure out what we're going to do."

"I already know what to do," Arak said. "So does Henry. And so should you."

***

Mihran called Teresa from a pay phone at the Atlantic Richfield station. He didn't want to take a chance that his mother might overhear the conversation.

Teresa responded to the news with silence.

"I just thought you ought to know," he said after a while.

"I suppose this raises the stakes."

"I guess so."

More silence.

"See you in the morning?" Mihran said. "We're still going to church, right?"

"Right," Teresa said. "Church. Tomorrow morning."

"I'll come by around 9:30."

***

The spot on the sidewalk normally reserved for the afternoon *Bee* was empty.

"When's the paper get here?" Mihran called out to the Gideon.

"Pretty soon." Gideon glanced at his watch and frowned. "They're usually here a little early on Saturdays. You going to have your name in the newspaper?"

"Nothing like that."

To keep his emotions in check, Mihran focused on the practical implications. Anaforian had said nothing about the man or his wife regaining consciousness or talking to the authorities. Logan would move quickly on the investigation, which meant Mihran would be talking with the detective soon. And then there were the Turks. What would they do now?

"What'd I tell you?" Gideon said.

A truck pulled up in front of the newsstand. A teenage boy tossed a stack of twine-bound newspapers through the open rear doors. The papers hit the sidewalk with a smack and skidded to a stop almost exactly in the spot Gideon had reserved for them. Mihran broke the string himself, grabbed a paper and left his nickel on the counter.

The story was on the front page, just below the fold:

Husband and Wife Die From Car Crash

But it was not the headline that captured Mihran's attention. It was the photograph. Looking back at him from the front page of the newspaper were the faces of Emin and Hazan Aybar and their infant daughter. The picture appeared to have been taken at a professional studio. The young couple sat side-by-side dressed in their finest clothes. Their daughter wore a fluffy dress with lots of frills, the kind of thing a little girl might put on for Easter or Christmas. She smiled at the camera from the comfort of her mother's lap. The girl's name, the caption said, was Fidan.

Mihran tried to read the article, but he could not make sense of the words. He closed his eyes, but the picture remained. Fidan Aybar. A little girl with a heartwarming smile. No more than a toddler. And now, an orphan.

Chapter Twenty-Six

Arak's head throbbed as he settled in behind the steering wheel. He had been up half the night replaying his conversation with Mihran. He wasn't terribly bothered by the fact that two people had died. He had considered the possibility all week and had long since convinced himself that the dead Turk was the one responsible for setting the events in motion. It was Mihran's reaction to the news that irritated him. Arak knew his brother would not betray him. But he also knew that Mihran would forever believe himself to be morally superior. Mihran was the one who cared, the one who cried over the Turks' deaths. It was Mihran who sacrificed his integrity to help the family, who saved his brother. Even Henry would think so.

"Maybe I should get a driver's license." Serena held two-year-old Eliz in her lap. Ana, two years older than her sister, sat in the back seat by herself. "Don't you think that's a good idea?"

"Why would you need a driver's license?"

"I don't like always having to depend on other people," Serena said. "If I had a license, I could drive myself around."

"And what would you drive?"

"This car," she said. "I could drive this car when you're not working or using it yourself."

"You don't need to drive anywhere," Arak said. "How many women you know drive?"

"Teresa does. She even has her own car."

"You're not Teresa."

"She's going be there this morning, you know," Serena said. "She's coming to church with Mihran. I told her they should come sit with us."

"Great. She going to convert, too?"

"If she wants to."

"Catholics never convert," Arak said. "Once that church gets you in its clutches, they never let go."

"How do you know what religion she is?"

"All Irish people are Catholic."

"And you don't like Teresa being Catholic?"

"I'm not thrilled with the idea."

"I guess you also don't like that she's part Mexican."

"That's not a problem if she doesn't make it one."

"How exactly would she go about making it a problem?"

"She just needs to keep it to herself, that's all."

"You wouldn't even know she was part Mexican if she hadn't said anything."

"Don't tell me about Mexicans." Arak glanced at the bruise on the side of his right hand, a reminder of his confrontation with the pickers at the pond. "I'm the one who works with them every day."

Eliz began to squirm, and Serena set her on the car seat next to Arak. Arak held his hand out in front of his daughter, who responded by wrapping her fingers around his thumb. Arak pulled lightly and pretended he couldn't get his thumb free. Eliz squealed with delight. She never tired of the game.

"It figures that Mihran would choose someone like her," Arak said.

"Someone like Teresa?" Serena said. "What about Teresa?"

"You know what I'm saying."

"I think she's a wonderful person."

"There are plenty of wonderful girls closer to home."

"You mean Teresa doesn't happen to be Armenian."

"There's no 'happens to be' about it," Arak said. "It's like Mihran *happens* to be working for someone other than Henry. Like he *happens* to be the only one in the family going to college."

"Maybe they just *happen* to love each other," Serena said. "You ever think of that?"

"Whatever you say."

"Would you have married me if I wasn't Armenian?"

"Don't be ridiculous."

***

Arak waited among the early arrivers in front of the church while Serena walked the girls to Sunday school. Sunshine radiating off the red brick facade promised another day of hundred-degree temperatures.

Babeg Bedrosian strolled up and shook Arak's hand. "A lot of people been talking about you this week. Down at the Asbarez Club, you've been the number one topic of conversation."

"And what are all these people saying?"

"First part of the week, they were all telling stories about how you tossed those Turks out of the picnic. I'm telling you, you were a legend."

"And after that?"

"Then that newspaper article came out," Babeg said. "The one about the Turks saying that the car crash was no accident."

"People believe that?"

"Who's going to believe anything a Turk says?" Babeg waved his hand as if to dismiss the thought. "But, you know. Some people get a little nervous. And then what happened yesterday."

"You mean, that they died?"

"Right." Babeg looked around. "Some people were wondering. Asking about what really happened. I mean, no one really knows anything. People are just asking. They're curious, is all."

"They think I'm to blame for the accident?"

"No, of course not," Babeg said. "Some people just don't know what to think. I mean, they all know what happened at the picnic. And then the car crashes. And then the Turks are dead."

"And what do you think?"

"I wouldn't believe anything coming out of a Turk's mouth. But, you know, people don't like what they're reading in the papers. They worry about what might happen next."

"You tell them nothing happens next," Arak said. "Tell them they're going to have to find someone else to talk about next week."

Chapter Twenty-Seven

The flicker of courage Teresa had been working on all morning disappeared as soon as she saw Mihran. The dark gray suit and white shirt made her more aware than ever of the contrast between his olive skin and black hair and her Irish features. He was a member of the Saropian family, on his way to Sunday church services where he would join rows of men and women with whom he shared physical characteristics. She could feel her confidence slipping with each approaching step.

"Great dress." Mihran held his fingers at angles as if taking in her appearance through a camera lens. She had settled on the viridian green after trying on several others that morning. Conservative without being boring.

"Is it too late to suggest brunch instead?" Teresa asked.

"You have no idea how many Armenians are eager to see you in your Sunday best."

"And eager to ask all those questions about marriage and children and what I plan to do with my college education anyway?"

"Sort of like the picnic last week, but with organ music and stained glass."

Mihran offered his arm. Teresa grabbed her purse.

In the car, she reminded herself that the service would be over in an hour, that the after-church socializing she had promised to participate in would be tolerable. But she could not deny the urge to leap from the vehicle at each stop sign. She could almost picture herself running in high heels past casually dressed pedestrians while Mihran's pleas to get back in the car became fainter and fainter behind her.

"You're awfully quiet this morning," he said.

"The priest," she said.

"Father Hoogasian. He's been there since I was a kid."

"What does he look like?"

"About sixty. A thick beard. Hair more gray than black these days."

"How tall is he?"

"Average. Or maybe a little shorter than average."

"What does he wear? A robe?"

"A black robe. Why?"

"Just getting prepared."

Soon the Holy Trinity Apostolic Church loomed in front of them. Teresa closed her eyes, but she could feel the presence of the structure as they drove past. Mihran pulled the car into the lot behind the church. He shut off the engine and rolled up his window.

"Shall we?"

Teresa sat quietly.

"You OK?" he asked.

"I don't think I can do this." The words slipped through her lips in a near-whisper.

"Can't do what?"

"The church," she said. "I don't think I can go."

"You feeling sick?"

"I'm sorry. I just can't."

"Is it about what happened to the Turks?"

"No. Nothing like that."

"You'll do fine. Everyone likes you, remember?"

"Not today." She clenched her hands into fists to keep them from shaking.

"I don't understand."

Teresa took a deep breath, exhaling slowly. She closed her eyes. She would not allow herself to have a panic attack. Not here. Not in front of Mihran.

"I said I was sorry."

"You don't need to apologize." Mihran rolled down his window. The light breeze that passed through the opening cooled the car. "I just want to know what's going on."

"That topic is not open for discussion."

He placed a hand on her shoulder. She shook it off.

"I said I'm not going."

"Sure," he said. "Whatever you want."

"You go in," she said. "I'll wait here in the car."

"Except that."

A young couple with two small boys walked past. A car pulled into the space next to them, and an elderly man and his wife stepped from the vehicle. It was almost time for the services to start.

"It's like this," Teresa said. "I'm afraid."

"Afraid of what people might say?"

"Not the people. It's the church."

He waited for an explanation.

"I know it's an irrational fear. A phobia. I know. It's crazy. I thought I could do it. But I can't."

"Is it something you want to talk about?" he asked.

There it was. She hadn't known how she would respond until this moment. The dozens of scripts she had written and rehearsed in her mind disappeared. She felt herself at a crossroads, that the choice she made right here and right now would send her down an irreversible path. She looked at Mihran and found nothing but sincerity in his eyes.

"I was abused," Teresa said.

"Abused? What happened?"

"Abused is a nice way of saying it. I was attacked. Which is another way of saying the truth. I was sexually assaulted."

"My God. When?"

"When I was thirteen."

"In a church?"

"In my church. My family's church. St. Anthony's."

Mihran reached for her, but she pulled her arms inward to stop him.

"There's more," Teresa said.

And then the words came pouring out. She told him everything in more detail than she thought possible. Father Hennessey, her plaid skirt, the dark hair on his arms, the smell of the recently waxed floor. When she was finished, he gently placed his hand on top of hers, where she allowed their fingers to slowly intertwine.

"Did you tell anyone?" Mihran asked.

"Just my mother."

"And what did she do?"

"She slapped me," Teresa said. "Hit me so hard it knocked me off my feet. She said I would rot in hell for telling such lies."

"Can I hold you?"

"Not at the moment."

"Sure."

She loved him for asking.

"I'm sure you always wondered why I don't get along with my mother." She found herself talking again. "And you know what? That part doesn't really bother me. Because I got to see her for who she really is. *She* turned her back on *me*. Better to have no mother than one like that."

The parking lot was quiet. The services had started.

"I've come a long way," Teresa said. "You should have seen me in high school. I've learned to deal with it. You have to. In a lot of ways, it makes you a stronger person."

Mihran squeezed her hand.

"You can hold me now," she said. "I want you to."

The breeze had disappeared, and the air inside the car was thick and hot. Their clothes were sticky with perspiration. But at that moment, as they wrapped their arms around one another, neither of them seemed to notice.

Chapter Twenty-Eight

With Serena in tow, Arak fused into the line of worshipers spilling out of the arched doorway and gathering on the expanse of sidewalk in front of the church.

Serena glanced about the crowd. "I don't know what happened to Mihran and Teresa. Mihran said for sure they would be here."

"Maybe she's not as keen on becoming a part of this family as you think," Arak said. "Why don't you go get the girls?"

Arak positioned himself at the bottom of the steps and did his best to make eye contact with the men and women passing by. He exchanged short greetings with a few families, but no one stopped to chat. Only Kemar, one of the men who had stood with Arak when he confronted the Turks at the picnic, made a point of shaking his hand. Yet even Kemar quickly excused himself, leaving Arak alone in front of the church.

The clamor of a dozen conversations was suddenly drowned out by the blare of a car horn. Arak turned to find two cars stopped in the middle of Ventura Avenue directly in front of the church. A large man with dark features sat in the front seat of a faded green Buick. He pounded out a series of long blasts on his horn while a second man waved a fist through the open back seat window. The lone man in the second car, a yellow sedan with a dent in the rear fender, tapped his horn in a staccato rhythm. Traffic came to a halt.

"Murderers," the fist-waving man shouted. "Justice for the victims! Killers go to jail, not to church!"

For a moment, no one knew how to react. Most of the church-goers stared at the spectacle, trying to make sense of the scene. People near the doorway stepped back inside the building.

One man pointed from the top of the steps. "It's those Turks. The ones from the picnic."

Arak felt a dozen eyes turn his way.

A red brick slammed into the side of the church. Chips flew, and the brick bounced a few times before landing with a high-pitched clunk on the sidewalk.

Suddenly everyone was in motion. There were gasps and screams. Parents hovered over their children. Others ran toward the parking lot.

One of the Turks stepped from his car and held another brick in the air. "No peace for murderers," he yelled. "No mercy!"

The second brick bounced off the front steps. People scrambled for cover. Children overwhelmed by the chaos began to cry.

The two cars sped off.

Arak stepped into the street and watched the vehicles disappear around the corner. When he turned back around, the sidewalk was deserted. The front doors to the church were closed, but a lone figure remained at the top of the steps. It was Father Hoogasian, who motioned for Arak to come to him.

"May I have a word with you?"

"I had nothing to do with this, Father," Arak said.

"Please come with me."

"Certainly, Father."

Arak followed the priest into a small, windowless room inside the building. Father Hoogasian closed the door behind them and remained standing. Although nearly seventy, he carried himself in a manner that demanded respect. His penetrating stare kept Arak still and silent.

"I do not know what provoked this incident," the priest said. "And I don't want to get involved in whatever dispute you have with these individuals."

"I'm as surprised and upset about it as anyone," Arak said.

"This is our church," Father Hoogasian said. "It is a holy place. It is the Lord's house."

"I understand, Father."

"It is not a place for arguments or violence."

"Absolutely, Father."

The priest stepped forward until he was inches from Arak's face. Arak understood that he was not to move.

"Don't ever bring this kind of thing here again."

Chapter Twenty-Nine

Talk around the table was more subdued than any Sunday dinner Henry could recall. Even the granddaughters, normally an endless source of energy, poked quietly at their plates at the other end of the table. Serena remarked on how quickly the girls grow out of their clothes. Mihran explained that Teresa had become ill that morning right before church. Tarvez offered extra helpings of everything. But conversations didn't go very far. Arak was especially quiet. When Henry finished his coffee, he asked his nephews to join him outside.

The three men gathered in a circle near the vegetable garden in the back yard. Even in the diminishing light, Henry could see that the lower leaves on the tomato plants were turning brown and that the tallest of the ranging plants had begun to sag under their own weight. Summer was in decline.

"This thing at church today," Henry said.

"I can't believe those bastards," Arak said.

"People are upset."

"We're all upset."

"I worry about where this is headed."

"Don't be," Arak said. "Those Turks are afraid to do anything but make noise. Did you see how quickly they drove away?"

"This needs to end," Henry said. "As soon as possible."

"They're the ones who showed up where they weren't welcome."

"They're angry."

"I'm angry."

Serena opened the back door. "Phone call. Uncle Henry, they're looking for you."

"Who is?" Henry asked.

"Mid-Valley Fire Department."

***

Henry parked his Cadillac behind the collection of fire trucks. The barn was in flames. Mihran and Arak leapt from the car, but Henry watched the scene through the open window. A torrent of orange and yellow rose into the black sky. Only the occasional crack of burning wood penetrated the roar of the fire. Except for a group spraying water from one of the trucks onto the roof of Arak's office, the firefighters stood in small circles watching. They were clad in dark protective gear, their exposed skin smudged and streaked with ash and perspiration. Several farmhands looked on from the perimeter.

"Mr. Saropian?" A man in a gray uniform identified himself as Captain Whitfield. "You're the legal owner of this structure?"

"It's mine." Henry stepped from the car and shook the captain's hand, but he could not take his eyes off the burning barn. "Or was mine. Can anything be saved?"

"When they're this far gone, we just try to keep them from spreading," Whitfield said. "As far as we can tell, there were no people or livestock in the barn. Does that sound right to you?"

"There shouldn't have been," Henry said. "A lot of tools and equipment, though. And a fairly new tractor."

The fire captain studied the burning building as if verifying Henry's statement. A sudden shift in the wind blasted them with a wave of heat. Several firefighters covered their faces and stepped back from the curling clouds of smoke.

"What about a cause?" Arak asked. "What can you tell us about that?"

"Nothing official," Whitfield said. "But in this case, it doesn't take an expert. We appear to have two places of origin in a building with no electricity. It's up to the inspector to call it arson. But a blind man could figure this one out."

The fire captain excused himself and barked some instructions to his men. They stopped spraying the office and started packing up equipment.

"Of course, a blind man could figure it out," Arak said. "Just like the crates and tools down by the pond. They want us to know it's no accident. Damned Mexicans."

"How do you know it's the Mexicans?" Mihran asked. "How do you know the Turks didn't do this? They found the church easily enough."

"Look around." Arak gestured with open arms. "You see any Mexicans anywhere? Don't you think they would find a fire like this interesting enough to come out and watch?"

Henry glanced around and discovered that Arak was right. Except for the farmhands, the fire had attracted no spectators.

"It's their way of telling us," Arak said. "They know all about the fire, including who started it. But come tomorrow, not a damned one of them is going to say a thing."

Leon Nazarian ran toward them. "Mr. Saropian, come look. Come look at this."

Leon led them to the office and pointed at the front door. The wet surface glistened in the orange light.

Arak bent forward and studied the door.

"Bullet holes," Arak said. "Four of them."

He stepped aside to let Henry examine the holes. Mihran followed.

"They would have got you," Leon said. "Look how high they are. If you'd have been in there at your desk, they would have got you."

"I'm sure the shooter knew the office was empty," Henry said.

"That's what you want to believe, isn't it?" Arak said.

"If they had wanted to shoot you, they would have waited until they knew you were in there," Henry said. "But they did this on a Sunday night."

"They're showing us how easy it would be." Arak turned to Mihran. "You're the bright one in the family. What do you think we ought to do, little brother?"

"We tell the police," Mihran said. "We let the officials handle it."

"And what do you think the police are going to do?" Arak asked. "None of these Mexicans are going to say anything. The cops will poke around a little. They'll come up with nothing and then forget about it."

"And you think you can figure out who did it?" Mihran asked.

"I already know who did it."

"And who would that be?"

"The pickers."

"All of them?"

"They all know who lit the match."

Henry stepped between the brothers. "Let's go inside and see the damage."

Henry unlocked the door and was pleased to find that the lights still worked. Neither the fire nor the fire fighters had affected the power lines. He closed the door behind them, leaving the sounds and smells of the fire outside.

"Leon was right." Arak fingered a bullet hole in the front of his wooden desk. "They were aiming at just about the perfect height."

"Better not touch that," Mihran said. "The police will want to look at it."

"Oh, right." Arak lifted his arm away in an exaggerated fashion. "The police."

"Knock it off, Arak."

"We're not telling the police about this," Henry said. "Not about the bullet holes."

"You're kidding," Mihran said.

"I don't want them asking the workers a lot of questions." Henry looked directly at Arak. "They might hear some stories we don't want the police to know about. Am I right, Arak?"

"You are," Arak said. "But tell me this doesn't change things."

Henry hated to make the concession. "I suppose it does."

"You're damned right it does."

"Listen to me," Henry said. "You are not going to go after anyone. No more retaliation. Is that clear?"

"If you say so," Arak said.

"This is the first time I've heard of a worker using a gun. We can't ignore that. But you need to be cautious."

"You know I will be."

"This is the exception to the rule, Arak."

"I know the rule."

"What are you two talking about?" Mihran asked.

"We're saying you can't just stick your head in the ground when someone's coming after you with a gun," Arak said.

"And what does that mean?" Mihran asked.

"I'll show you."

Arak grabbed a letter opener from the desktop and stepped to the corner of the room where he pried a loose board from the floor just under the wash basin. He pulled a long cardboard box from the opening and carried it back to the desk. Mihran leaned in as Arak lifted a stained yellow cloth from the box and then unfurled the cloth to reveal a rifle.

"Jesus," Mihran said in a half-whisper. "How long has that been there?"

"This is a farm," Arak said. "We're a long way from the nearest police station."

Arak unwrapped a second object. Another rifle, identical to the first.

"Remington 22," Arak said. "Not a lot of firepower. But enough. One for the office, one for home."

"Are you crazy?" Mihran said.

"Nobody is planning to shoot anybody," Henry said. "This is for protection only."

Arak aimed one of the rifles at an imaginary target. "Does this scare you, little brother? A little afraid of firearms, maybe?"

"I carried a rifle in Korea," Mihran said. "Remember?"

"But did you ever use it?"

"Of course."

"Did you ever shoot at anyone?"

"I saw combat."

"What about ammunition?" Henry asked.

Arak moved to the opening in the floor and pulled out a small box of bullets. He held the box at eye level and smiled at his uncle.

"You need to be smart," Henry said. "The pickers will be gone in a couple of days. And I expect you to do everything possible to see that they are the most uneventful days we've ever had around here."

"Absolutely," Arak said. "I'd like nothing better myself."

"I mean it, Arak. Self-defense only."

"Of course." Arak rewrapped one of the rifles and returned it to the hiding place under the wash basin. "Self-defense only."

Chapter Thirty

Serena was asleep by the time Arak got home. He went to the kitchen to pour himself a much-needed drink, which he carried with him while he checked and rechecked each window and the locks on each door. As he often did during this nightly ritual, he stopped in the doorway of the girls' room to take in the sight of his two daughters sleeping in the muted light. Ana and Eliz. Each named after a great grandmother. He had picked the names himself, and Serena knew there would be no point in disagreeing.

He stepped to Ana's bed and studied his little girl. Others didn't see it, but somewhere in the face Arak recognized his mother's features. The birth of his first daughter had been the most important event in his life. It was the day he joined generations of Saropian men and accepted the responsibility that comes with fatherhood. From that point on, it was up to him to protect, guide and provide for this child. That was more than four years ago, the day he started a new branch on the family tree.

He moved to Eliz's bed, where he spent a few minutes watching his two-year-old until the weight of a very difficult day pushed him toward sleep. Arak finished the last of his drink and paused to say a silent prayer. He thanked God for blessing him with these two wonderful girls.

***

Mihran was surprised to discover the lights were still on. He found his mother sitting at the kitchen table sipping a cup of tea.

"I thought you'd be asleep," Mihran said.

"Soon," Tarvez said. "How is the barn?"

"Gone." Mihran poured himself a cup and joined her at the table. "Nothing could be saved. But at least the fire didn't spread."

"Anyone hurt?"

"Just property damage."

"Do they know the cause?"

"A fire inspector will check it out. Probably in the morning."

Tarvez nodded. "Have you heard from Teresa?"

Mihran held back a smile. His mother had not stayed up to hear about the fire. He had explained to everyone that Teresa didn't feel well. But now it was just the two of them, and if there was more to the story, his mother wanted to know.

"Teresa's fine," he said. "She needs to be. Tomorrow's the first day of classes."

"Be careful with her."

"I thought you liked Teresa."

"I do," Tarvez said. "What I mean is, she's a lot more fragile than she lets on."

"I'm discovering that."

"You know she doesn't have to attend a church service."

"Why wouldn't she?"

"Church is not for everyone," Tarvez said. "I hope she knows it's not a family requirement."

"I'm sure she does. Maybe next week."

"Maybe."

Mihran gathered their empty cups and rinsed them in the sink. When he saw that his mother had not moved, he knew to return to his place at the table.

"Mihran, do you believe in God?"

"Why would you ask such a question?"

"I see you in church," Tarvez said. "You don't pray. You lower your head a little, but you don't close your eyes."

"Not much gets by you," he said. "But tell me. How would you know what I'm doing during prayer when you're supposed to be praying yourself?"

Tarvez grinned. "Always my clever one."

It was an unexpected tender moment, the kind they often shared when he was a child and could not sleep at night. He always found comfort in her late-night words. Even when he couldn't follow the message, her quiet confidence reassured him that there were answers out there. Giving up those moments had been a steep price to pay for becoming an adult.

"It's funny," Mihran said. "I don't remember the two of us ever having a discussion about religion. We always went to church. But that just seemed like a given. Like going to work or going to school."

"There's more to church than religion."

"That's what I've been trying to tell Teresa."

"So do you?" Tarvez asked. "Believe?"

He smiled at her tenacity. "What do you mean by *believe*?"

"What a perfect answer." Tarvez could not hold back a laugh. "That's just what I would expect you to say."

"It's not a simple question."

"It is for most people. But, of course, it wouldn't be for you."

"Sorry."

"Don't be," Tarvez said. "It's one of your best qualities."

"Let's say I'm still studying the matter."

The answer seemed to satisfy her.

"Now it's your turn," Mihran said. "Do you believe?"

Tarvez nodded as if she should have expected the question. "My relationship with God is not so easy to put into words."

"You see?"

"God and I have been through a lot together."

Tarvez looked past him for a moment. She seemed to be taking the question much more seriously than he had intended.

"You know, it's not the things God does that are hard to understand," she said. "It's what he chooses not to do. That's the other side of being all powerful."

There was no need to ask. They both understood what she was talking about.

"I've been told my survival was a miracle," Tarvez said. "Do you think it was a miracle?"

"It could be."

"But you don't believe in miracles."

"To be honest, probably not."

"I think I once did," she said. "When I was a child."

"And now?"

"Now I think if God had wanted to help me..." She paused to take a deep breath. "If he had wanted to help, then he surely would have done so earlier."

Chapter Thirty-One

Mihran studied his features in the bathroom mirror and tried to get his mind around the fact that in a few hours he once again would be sitting in a college classroom. The world of books, chalkboards and essays was far removed from the one where barns are burned to the ground, bricks are thrown at churches, and a young couple can die over an exchange of angry words from decades-old tensions.

He was collecting his things and about to head out when someone knocked on the front door. As he moved to answer it, Mihran thought about how Anaforian had pounded on the door two days earlier and about the phone call from the fire department the previous night. It seemed news these days was always bad.

"Mihran Saropian?"

Even before the man introduced himself, Mihran knew the visitor had to be Officer Logan. He invited the police detective inside. Anaforian was not with him.

"I spoke with your brother Arak a few nights ago," Logan said. "I wonder if you have a few minutes for some questions."

"I was just on my way to the college," Mihran said. "Fall classes start today."

"I won't take much of your time."

Mihran motioned for Logan to sit on the couch. He closed the door to the kitchen before taking a seat himself. As he watched Logan open his thin notebook, Mihran felt a surprising sense of relief. He knew what he had to say. And if he did his part, this entire episode could soon be behind him.

"I hear you had some trouble outside the courthouse last week," Logan said.

"That's right." Mihran was a little taken aback by the question. He had given the policeman his name at the time, but no official report had been filed.

"You want to tell me about that?"

"Nothing much came of it," Mihran said. "I ran away from some people who were trying to hurt me. The police broke things up. I don't remember the name of the officer I talked to."

"Officer Slaton," Logan said.

"I guess you talked with him."

"So you're saying they started it?"

"I was attacked and outnumbered. I just wanted to get out of there."

"Why did they attack you?"

"I'm not entirely sure," Mihran said. "I was minding my own business. Heading back to work after dropping something off for my boss."

"A group of people attack you for no apparent reason, and you don't bother trying to find out why?"

"I have an idea."

"Which is?"

"There was an article in the paper the next day about some Turkish college students," Mihran said. "I think they might be the same people who showed up at the Armenian picnic the previous Sunday. Or at least some of them were the same."

"But why would they want to hurt you?"

"There was a car accident the night of the picnic. Some of their friends were killed, and, according to the paper, somehow they think someone from the picnic might be responsible."

"Someone," Logan said. "*Someone* might be responsible. You have no idea who that someone is?"

"I don't know anything about the accident."

"You think your brother was involved in the accident?"

"Not at all." The words came out quickly, but, Mihran thought, with confidence. There would be no turning back now.

"How can you be so sure?"

"Because Arak and I rode home from the picnic together," Mihran said. "But if you talked with Arak, you already know that."

"The Turks at the courthouse," Logan said. "You ever seen them before?"

"I can't be sure. But they could have been some of the people at the picnic."

"Can't be sure," Logan said. "They didn't say anything? They just quietly started beating on you?"

"They yelled some things."

"Such as?"

"One of them thought he remembered me from the picnic."

"Now we're getting somewhere." Logan tapped his notepad with his pencil. "So you talked to them at the picnic?"

"No," Mihran said. "Arak talked to them. But I didn't."

"But you were there?"

"A lot of people were standing around. I was one of them."

"Then you heard what your brother told the Turks?"

"Most of it."

"So you heard him threaten the Turks."

"I didn't hear any threats," Mihran said. "They were simply asked to leave. Arak told them they weren't welcome."

"Not welcome? Why not?"

"I don't think I need to tell you why Turks don't belong at an Armenian picnic."

"Because Armenians hate Turks. Is that it?"

"Let's say we don't get along."

"What would have happened to the Turks if they had come back to the next picnic?"

"They would have been asked to leave."

"And if they didn't?"

"That's not a likely scenario," Mihran said. "People don't usually go where they're not wanted."

"Scenario." Logan straightened his posture in mock admiration. "Not a likely *scenario*."

Mihran let it pass.

"You seem to know a lot about these Turkish students," Logan said.

"Just what I've read in the newspaper."

"And what have you learned from the newspaper?"

"What I've already told you," Mihran said. "Some Turkish students think there's more to the car accident than meets the eye."

"Two people died in that accident. Did you know that?"

"Yes, I was very sorry to read that."

"Sorry? Why?"

"Because some people died. There was a picture in the *Fresno Bee.* They had a little girl."

"And that upsets you?"

"It should upset anyone."

"They were Turks."

"They were people."

"You know the names of the Turks who died?"

The names immediately came to mind. Emin and Hazan Aybar. "I'm sure it was in the paper, but I don't recall the names."

"Then do you know the name of the Turk who went to the *Bee* and said he wanted an investigation?" Logan asked. "You saw that story, right?"

"I saw the story," Mihran said. "But no, I don't recall the name."

"Probably the same guy who attacked you at the courthouse, wouldn't you say?"

"I don't know."

"You don't know?" Logan lifted his eyebrows to create an exaggerated expression of disbelief. "If a man attacked me, accused my brother of murder, then went to the D.A.'s office and the newspaper demanding an investigation. You know, I think I might be a little curious about who that person was and why he was doing all these things."

"I read the stories. I just don't recall the name."

"You mean to tell me, Armenians aren't talking among themselves about these Turks and the accident?"

"Probably, but I've not been involved in those conversations."

"I hear some Turks showed up at your church yesterday," Logan said. "Are you going to tell me you didn't talk about it afterward?"

"I wasn't there yesterday."

"Now that's interesting. Why not?"

"Something came up," Mihran said.

Logan waited for Mihran to elaborate. Mihran waited for Logan to continue.

"If there's nothing else, I need to get to class," Mihran said.

"Do you think I care whether you miss class?" Logan said.

"Probably not."

"You don't seem too concerned that your brother is being accused of causing a fatal accident."

"Because I know he wasn't involved."

"You haven't by chance been talking to Officer Anaforian about any of this, have you?"

"No."

"You know Officer Anaforian?"

"Sure. I've known him since before he joined the police force."

"And you're saying you did *not* talk to Officer Anaforian?"

"Not about the accident."

"You willing to say that under oath?"

"It's the truth."

Another moment of silence.

"Tell me what happened after the picnic," Logan said.

"I rode home with Arak," Mihran said. "We stopped at Vincent's grocery store out on the highway and bought some cigarettes. Then we drove home."

"You drive down Clovis Avenue?"

"Arak drove. And yes, we came down Clovis Avenue."

"You see the accident?"

"No."

"But if the Turks left the picnic before you did, the accident would have happened before you got there. You didn't see the police cars? The ambulance? Any of that?"

"Nothing at all."

"How do you explain that?"

"I don't know when the accident happened," Mihran said. "But I saw no evidence of it when we drove that stretch of road. Maybe it happened later. Maybe the Turks stopped somewhere after the picnic."

"You see anyone at the grocery store?"

"Just the owner, Vincent."

"Anybody else?"

"Not that I recall."

"You didn't see the Turks there?"

"No," Mihran said. "I would have remembered that."

"Arak didn't talk to Vincent about the Turks?"

"He might have," Mihran said. "He and I were still talking about what happened at the picnic."

"So he was upset?"

"He didn't like the Turks showing up."

"And what did he say to Vincent?"

"I don't remember exactly," Mihran said. "Something about how he hoped Vincent didn't have to do business with any Turks. Something like that."

"Because he saw the Turks in the store?"

"I told you, we didn't see the Turks."

"How about outside the store? Maybe in the parking lot?"

"After we left the picnic, we didn't see any Turks anywhere that night."

Logan slapped his notebook closed and rose to his feet.

"I think you're lying," Logan said. "I think your brother's a liar, too. And I think you just got yourself into a whole lot of trouble. What do you think of that?"

Mihran shrugged. "I can only tell you the truth."

"We'll see." Logan moved quickly to leave.

Mihran stood in the open doorway and watched the police detective drive away. He knew he had done well. But he also knew that he would revisit the scene many times. How he would eventually come to see it and himself as a result of what he had done, he could not guess.

Chapter Thirty-Two

The call from Anaforian had sounded urgent. Mihran excused himself just as he and Tarvez were sitting down to dinner. He met Arak in front of the house, and the two brothers quickly made their way, as instructed, to the parking lot in front of Kevorkian's Garage on Inyo Street. Mihran had no desire to speculate about what Anaforian might have to tell them, and he was pleased that Arak offered no guesses as they walked to the meeting place largely in silence.

The lot was empty except for a single car parked in front of the closed garage door. Anaforian stepped from the vehicle as the brothers approached. He looked smaller out of uniform, more like a guy who sold shoes than a policeman. The expression on his face was impossible to read. When Mihran extended a hand, Anaforian pulled him forward, grabbed him around the neck, and pretended to rub his knuckles into the top of Mihran's head.

"Your brother did good," Anaforian said to Arak.

"What's he done now?" Arak asked.

"The way he talked to Logan." Anaforian released Mihran but gave him a punch in the arm as they separated. "Said everything just right. Logan worked him hard. But Mihran didn't budge."

"So where does that leave us?" Arak asked.

"Leaves you free and clear," Anaforian said. "Logan's got no choice. Between you and me, I don't think he believes a goddamned thing anyone's telling him. But what's he going to do?"

"Then it's over?" Arak said. "No more investigation?"

"Single-car accident," Anaforian said. "Case closed. Logan's making it official tomorrow morning."

"What about Vincent?" Mihran asked.

163

"Vincent didn't see a damned thing," Anaforian said. "He just remembered Arak saying something about Turks. That's all. Thought you *might* have run into them. But he didn't see a damned thing."

Arak shook the policeman's hand. "When this blows over, I am going to buy you a nice dinner, sir. And maybe even a drink or two to celebrate."

"Why wait?" Anaforian said. "You ever been to Roselyn's Steak-house?"

"Where's that?"

"Kingsburg." Anaforian opened the door to his car. "Nobody will know us there. Hop in. We can be at Roselyn's in forty-five minutes."

***

Arak ordered bourbon on the rocks for all of them. He and Anaforian finished their drinks in a few gulps and ordered a second round when the waitress returned to take their food order. The two had sat in the front seat laughing and telling jokes all the way to the restaurant. Mihran sipped his bourbon slowly. It did not feel like an occasion to celebrate.

"Hey, little brother." Arak lifted his glass. "Join in the fun."

"I think I'll wait until I get a little food in me," Mihran said.

Anaforian held his glass next to Arak's. "How about a toast for that Logan? What a detective, huh?"

"What about the Turks?" Mihran asked. "Do they know yet?"

"Logan's going to tell them tomorrow," Anaforian said.

"I'd like to be there for that," Arak said.

"They'll be pissed," Anaforian said. "No doubt about it."

"You really think that's going to be the end of it?" Mihran asked.

"Logan's going to tell them." Anaforian finished his second drink and signaled the waitress to bring two more. "We rely on evidence in this country. And they ain't got any. Case closed."

"What if they go to the newspaper?" Mihran asked. "They did before."

"Let 'em," Anaforian said. "They talk to the reporter. The reporter talks to Logan. Logan tells him there's no evidence of any wrongdoing. And then what? If they get any kind of story at all, it'll be how there's nothing to their accusations."

"Damned right," Arak said. "Cheer up, Mihran. We won this time."

"They'll still think we're responsible for the accident," Mihran said.

"Piss on them," Arak said.

"Who knows what they're capable of?" Mihran said. "They already came after me once. And then there's that stuff at the church."

"You're forgetting who we're dealing with here." Arak set his glass on the table with a thud, a sign that he was feeling the liquor. "These are Turks. They throw a brick, and then they run."

"They're not wanted around here," Anaforian said. "Maybe they'll see that now. Maybe they'll decide it's time to leave this valley. Hell, it's time for them to leave this country."

"Damned right," Arak said. "What are they doing in Fresno anyway?"

"You know where they live?" Anaforian said. "You know those old houses out on Peach? Just south of Shaw?"

"Dick Somervel's old farm?"

"That's it," Anaforian said. "There's three or four of these old shacks out there where the farm workers used to stay. Look like they've been there a hundred years. A good gust of wind would blow the damned things right over. I mean, the goddamned pickers wouldn't even stay there anymore."

"That's where they live?" Arak said. "In those old shacks?"

"Hey, we're talking about Turks. A bunch of peasants. I'd be surprised if they had indoor plumbing."

"Did you go there? Did you go inside?"

"Logan wanted to talk to them alone. They'd really shit their pants if they had to talk to a cop named Anaforian."

"Anafor - ee - an," Arak said, drawing out the last two syllables.

"Anafor - ee - an," the police officer repeated.

They both burst into laughter.

"I bet they aren't even paying rent," Anaforian said. "Probably just squatting like a bunch of gypsies. I ought to run their asses out of there."

"No," Arak said. "Let the roof collapse on them. While they're sleeping. Then we mail their flattened bodies back to Turkey in an envelope."

Another huge laugh.

"You don't think that's funny?" Arak asked Mihran.

"I'm just not sure this is over," Mihran said. "I can't see them going away quietly."

"You think too much, little brother," Arak said. "That's why you could never do my job. You want to believe you're too smart to work on a farm. But the truth is, you'd spend the whole day thinking instead of doing."

"Why don't you lighten up on the liquor until you've had something to eat?" Mihran said.

"Nothing would ever get done," Arak said. "Think. Think. Think. In the real world, you have to make decisions."

Mihran could feel his anger rising. He glanced toward the kitchen hoping to see the waitress approaching with their meals.

"I'm telling you," Arak said. "Good judgment is a hell of a lot more important than any of that crap you learn in college."

"Like the good judgment you showed on Clovis Avenue after the picnic?" Mihran said.

Arak slammed a fist on the table top. "What I did, I did for you and for every Armenian in the valley."

"What you did, you did for yourself."

Anaforian stood halfway out of his chair and extended his arms between the brothers. "Easy guys. This is not the place."

Mercifully, the waitress arrived with their food. For several minutes, the three men ate in silence.

"We're all in this together," Arak said in a low voice. "You made some decisions yourself."

"I did what you and Henry wanted me to," Mihran said.

"You having second thoughts about that?"

"I did what I had to do. There's no taking it back."

"Same with me."

Mihran finished his drink. "And now we both have to live with it."

Chapter Thirty-Three

Henry removed his hat before knocking. He had waited until dark, hoping he would not be seen. Sounds coming from nearby closed doors told him that he had managed to arrive before bedtime.

The unpainted door screeched open on rusty hinges. Roberto blinked twice. "Mr. Saropian."

"They told me this was where you were staying," Henry said. "May I come in?"

"Of course."

It had been many years since Henry had been inside one of the migrant shacks. The room was even smaller than he remembered. Nearly half the space was taken up by the single bed. A portable lamp hanging from the low ceiling provided the only light. There was no window.

"Just you?" Henry asked.

"My wife passed away three years ago," Roberto said. "My boys are grown and have families of their own. They don't pick fruit anymore. They got other jobs."

"It's been two years since I lost my wife," Henry said. "We had no children."

Roberto gestured for Henry to sit on the bed. He waited until Henry had settled onto the stained blanket covering the thin mattress before turning a wooden crate on its side to create his own place to sit.

"You are surprised to see me?" Henry said.

"Yes, sir. Is there something wrong?"

Henry detected a faint smell of fried meat and onions. A muffled conversation in Spanish could be heard through the wall.

167

"You've been coming here for quite a few years now, haven't you?" Henry said.

"Yes, sir. I would say twenty or maybe even twenty-five years."

"And you have been working on farms even longer?"

"Since I was a boy."

"I picked fruit as a boy," Henry said. "Grapes, mostly. Some peaches and apricots. And figs. Me and my brother. Of course, we didn't have to move around like you."

The lamp cast everything in the room in the same amber hue. The light softened the weather-worn features on Roberto's face and, Henry noticed when he glanced at his own hands, had the same effect on his aging skin.

"I think every farm owner should spend some time working in the fields," Henry said. "I mean, real work. I know some owners who have never picked for more than a few hours at a time. It's different being out there every day. Or being out there because you have to."

"Yes, sir."

"My father had to," Henry said. "He took whatever work he could get. Cleared fields, dug up stumps, strung barbed wire. And my mother. She got work at Del Monte during packing season. Worked as many hours as they would give her. Me and my brother Bedros stayed with the neighbors. Some nights we were already asleep when she'd come to get us."

"My father was the fastest picker I ever saw," Roberto said. "He could finish two rows in the time it took some men to pick just one. I wanted to be just like him. But it was not the life he wanted for his children. He said he would quit someday, as soon as something better came along. He said someday we would stop moving with the crops. Someday we would have a place of our own."

"My father always talked about buying his own farm." It occurred to Henry that he had not revealed this fact to anyone before. He had never wanted to make his father seem sad or foolish. "He had it all figured out. He was going to have a vineyard, of course. But also melons, peaches, cherries. And, for my mother, a pomegranate tree. Just outside the kitchen window, he would tell her. And she always acted like she believed him. We would pass farmhouses, and they would talk about what they liked about this one or that one and what they would do different when they built their house. I realize now that she was just playing along. Maybe they both were."

"My father died when he was thirty-nine," Roberto said. "Pneumonia. He was in the back seat of the car, and we were on our way to the apple orchards up north. I was barely old enough, but I was driving. My mother was sitting next to him. She knew he was gone long before we arrived. But she said nothing until we got there."

"And you kept working on farms?"

"What else could I do? I had a mother and three sisters."

"I had a mother and a little brother," Henry said. "I was fourteen. I quit school and went to work. Some of the cousins helped us a little. When they could."

"Family is very important," Ricardo said.

"It is."

Ricardo's personal possessions were arranged in neat rows across the top of a wooden crate at the foot of the bed. From where he sat, Henry could see a glass, a razor, a bar of soap, a book of matches, a folded towel, a metal plate and a few utensils. There was also a small metal cross and a framed black and white photograph of a woman standing in front of a church.

"You have the respect of the other pickers," Henry said.

"I like to think so. They come to me sometimes when they need help."

"Because you are the oldest?"

"There are older men here," Roberto said. "I like to think it is how I act. A man must earn respect."

"That is very true."

"And you, Mr. Saropian. I believe you are such a man for your people."

"I suppose I am."

"I am pleased that you came to see me tonight, Mr. Saropian," Roberto said. "Is there something that I can do for you?"

"There is." The question pulled Henry back to the business that had brought him here. "This thing with Enrico."

"We took care of that." Roberto seemed uncomfortable with the new topic. "The night we learned what happened, we told the three men to leave."

"I heard they were injured."

"Two of them were."

"So injured that they were unable to work?"

"They could still do some work," Roberto said. "Enrico has his wrist in a cast. But he can pick with one hand for a while. Serge, the young one. He broke two fingers. He can still use both hands, but he is not so fast with them anymore."

"There must have been medical expenses."

"We had enough money for the doctors."

"You paid for it?"

"Everybody gave a little," Roberto said. "This is how we are. We take care of our people. We may not have much, but we work together. That is something that makes me proud. I believe you would understand this, Mr. Saropian. Your people also take care of each other, do they not?"

"We do indeed."

A quiet moment signaled that their conversation was coming to an end.

"I am sorry for what those men did," Roberto said. "They are young. It is different these days for young men. Some are angry. They think hurting people is the way to use their anger."

"I see that in some of our young people," Henry said.

"But they are gone. They will not be coming back. I promise, nothing like that will ever happen again."

"Can you tell me, when did they leave?"

"The very next day. The day after they were hurt. Two of them went to a doctor, and then they were gone."

"Before the fire?"

Roberto looked puzzled. "The fire at the barn? They were gone before that."

"Are you sure? Maybe they were still in the area."

"Those men had nothing to do with the fire. They were far away. They were not coming back."

"Could it have been other pickers?"

"No, sir," Roberto said. "None of the pickers would burn the barn."

"How do you know?"

"I would know. If one of them had started the fire, I would know."

"And the bullet holes in the office?"

"You mean a gun?" Roberto was taken aback by the suggestion. "No, sir. No gun. No one would carry a gun. I have never seen anyone with a gun."

"Maybe one of the young men?" Henry asked.

"Believe me, Mr. Saropian," Roberto said. "There is no gun."

"I do believe you, Roberto."

Henry allowed a respectful moment to pass before rising. "I suppose I should be going."

"Thank you, Mr. Saropian."

Henry touched his hand to his pants pocket where he felt the money he had intended to give Roberto. He left the folded stack of dollars where it was. As he shook the other man's hand, Henry realized with a sense of regret that he had failed to do so upon his arrival.

"Good night, Roberto."

"Good night, Mr. Saropian."

Chapter Thirty-Four

Mihran waited until his mother had gone to bed before closing the door to the kitchen and phoning Teresa.

"We just got word," Mihran said. "They're ending the investigation. They're calling it a single-car accident."

"So I guess that's good news," Teresa said.

"Of course."

"You talked with the detective?"

"A couple of days ago."

"I suppose I don't have to ask."

"You mean, what I told the detective?" he asked. "Look, you said you wanted this to end. And now it's over."

"And you're just fine with that?"

"I'm not pleased with anything. It was a bad situation all around. Not just bad. Terrible. Tragic. What can I say?"

"I just keep thinking about that family. About the little girl."

"I do, too."

"But you stood up for your brother."

"I did what I had to do."

"And was justice served?"

"Probably not," Mihran said. "But what do you want? You want someone in prison? Would that do any good?"

"I wonder what you would say if they hadn't been Turks," Teresa said. "How would you feel if Arak had run an Irish couple off the road?"

"If it had been an Irish couple, there wouldn't have been any trouble in the first place."

"You're avoiding my point."

"OK, sure. Maybe it makes a difference that they were Turks."

"That's the problem," Teresa said. "The more I think about this, the more it upsets me. And then when those people died."

"Let's not forget who killed millions of Armenians. Doesn't that mean anything?"

"It wasn't those two Turks. And it wasn't their daughter."

"Maybe you have to be Armenian to understand."

"I think that's what worries me."

"What are you saying?"

"Mihran, I'm glad you're not in trouble."

"But?"

"I love you. You know that. But this whole thing, it's made me think. I guess what I'm saying is that I'm just not sure I want to be a part of it."

"I told you, the case is closed. It's over."

"I'm not talking just about the car accident."

"I see." Mihran said. "Look, we can't resolve this on the phone. Are we still on for tomorrow night?"

"I don't know."

"Can I call you?"

"I think I need some time."

Chapter Thirty-Five

The knock on the door came just as Henry was sitting down to a dinner of broiled lamb and white bean *plaki*. His cooking skills had become a secret source of pride. After Katarine's death, he had gotten by largely on fried eggs and toast. But if life had taught Henry anything, it was how to respond to a challenge. Babeg, who himself had been widowed a few years earlier, had shown Henry how to prepare rice, wheat pilaf and a few vegetables. He figured out on his own how to fry, broil and bake various cuts of meat. There were some barely edible and a few completely inedible mistakes along the way, but he had survived. He even took a measure of satisfaction in acknowledging that his cooking would never be as good as Katarine's. Another reminder that his wife could never be replaced.

He opened the door to a stout man in a plain brown suit. The man's jacket was unbuttoned, and the knot in his tie was loose.

"Henry Saropian?"

Henry nodded.

"Timothy Morgan. Detective with the Sheriff's Department. May I come in?"

"Of course."

Henry took an immediate dislike to the man. Morgan started through the doorway before Henry could fully step aside. He slid his feet along the carpet rather than lift them properly, and he dropped his large frame onto the couch before Henry had invited him to sit.

"It's about the fire on your property the other night," Morgan said. "The one that destroyed your barn."

"What have you discovered?"

"An investigator from the Fire Marshall's Office was over to your property. Took him about two minutes to determine that it was arson."

"The fire chief thought so, too."

"Don't know why they think they always need a fire inspector," Morgan said. "This one was pretty basic. Whoever it was just threw gas or some other flammable on the back side of the barn and lit a couple of matches. The kind of thing amateurs do. Effective, though. An old wood structure like that barn of yours. Goes up pretty fast."

Morgan snapped his fingers to emphasize the point.

"So does the inspector have a suspect?" Henry asked. "A lead?"

"That's my job. But I got to tell you, there's not much to go on. No witnesses. Which figures. There's also no empty gas can with fingerprints on it, and there's about a million different footprints in the area. You want me to do something, I got to have something to work with, don't I?"

"Where does that leave us?"

"We look for people with motives." Morgan leaned back on the couch and crossed his legs, a pose that struck Henry as less than professional. "You tell me, Mr. Saropian. Who would want to burn your barn?"

"I have no idea." The words came out of his mouth so quickly they startled Henry.

"Anyone got a beef with you or your farm? Maybe a business rival or an employee you fired recently?"

"No one like that. Not that I know of anyway."

"What about the migrants?" Morgan asked. "We're seeing a lot more angry pickers these days. You had any problems with any of your pickers this year?"

"No." Henry shook his head slowly. "None at all."

"Then I got to tell you." The detective pointed a finger at Henry as if delivering a lecture. "Unless a witness comes forward, or unless there's another incident, there's not much more we can do. I mean, it's just property damage. It's not like someone was killed. Hell, you people own half the farmland around here anyway. One barn probably doesn't mean a whole lot. My advice is to cash the insurance check and keep your eyes open."

"Sounds like good advice."

Henry followed the detective to the door. Morgan paused in the open doorway.

"If I had to guess, I'd say it's one of the pickers," Morgan said. "They got no respect for personal property. All they own is what they can stuff in one of those old cars they drive. You about done with them for this season?"

"As a matter of fact, they're leaving tomorrow."

"Then I'd say you got nothing to worry about."

Chapter Thirty-Six

Henry parked his Cadillac alongside the migrants' partially loaded cars. The final row of grapes had been picked the previous afternoon, and the full-time farmhands would handle the rest of the rolling and packing and shipping over the next few days. Families scurried around with arms full of clothes, food, blankets, pots and pans, and whatever possessions the spaces in their cars allowed. Small children who had been nearly invisible during working days were suddenly everywhere.

It was a day of transition, from the busiest part of the year to the quietest. The clouds that had lingered on the horizon most of the week promised cooler weather ahead. Getting the dried grapes off the ground before the September rains would be the final concern before bringing picking season to a close.

Henry watched Roberto struggle with a bulging cardboard box. The small man let out a groan as he positioned the heavy box into the last remaining spot in the back of a beat-up gray truck. The old pickup had patches of oxidized paint on the hood and a sizable dent in the back fender. The rear sagged on what were obviously an exhausted set of springs. Like all the other migrant cars, the truck was covered with dust.

Roberto, his forehead gleaming with perspiration, slammed the tailgate closed and seemed surprised to find Henry standing a few feet away when he turned around.

"Good morning, Roberto." Henry extended his hand, which Roberto shook without hesitation.

"Good morning, Mr. Saropian."

Henry motioned toward the pickup. "Quite a load for one man."

"Most of it does not belong to me," Roberto said. "Some of the families. They barely got enough room for the kids. So I help them out."

"Leaving soon?"

"The truck is full. It is time to go."

Neither man moved.

"I want to thank you," Henry said. "For everything."

"It is a pleasure to work for a man like you," Roberto said.

"We will see you next year then."

"God willing."

They shook hands again. Henry watched as Roberto screeched open the pickup door, slid onto the seat, and drove away. He stood next to the vacated spot for several minutes and listened to the sounds of people on the move. People with lives very different from his, but with the same bonds between them that he knew with his own family and his own community. He had wanted to ask Roberto about the woman in the photograph. His late wife? Perhaps his mother or a sister? But he feared the question might have seemed intrusive, and what business was it of his anyway? Roberto had placed the picture next to his bed for his own reasons, not as a display for visitors.

"I'll be glad when the last one drives off." The voice came from behind him. Henry turned to find Arak standing with his arms folded across his chest.

"Picking season has been hell this year," Arak said.

"Most of them of good people," Henry said. "Hard workers."

"The older ones maybe."

Henry stepped away from the vehicles and motioned for Arak to join him.

"I want you to be careful," Henry said. "Stay on guard."

"I don't think they'll try anything on the last day," Arak said.

"I'm not talking about the migrants."

"What have you heard?"

"Nothing in particular."

"You know who set the barn on fire?"

"No, I don't."

Arak eyed his uncle. "But you don't think it was the Mexicans."

"I just want you to keep your eyes open."

"If there's trouble, I'm ready to take care of it."

"Trouble is what I want to avoid."

"You know if I can, I will."

Chapter Thirty-Seven

The building was not at all what Mihran had imagined. He had expected an impressive structure, an intimidating facade with intricate carvings. Perhaps a minaret or two. But the address took him to what appeared to be a renovated suite of offices on a largely residential street. A bronze plaque near the front door embedded with the star and crescent was the only outward indication that the building was indeed a mosque.

Mihran parked far enough down the block that he would not be noticed by anyone entering or leaving. He could not explain what he was doing here because he was not sure himself. The idea had been working its way through his awareness the past few days, since the article in the newspaper about the bereaved family of the accident victims. The funerals had been delayed a few days so that relatives could travel to the area to grieve with their loved ones.

By design, he had arrived after the services started. There was no shade to be found, and he rolled down all four car windows with the hope of catching a mid-morning breeze. He slouched behind the steering wheel and considered how all the optimistic beliefs he had constructed over the past several days had been eliminated one by one. *The accident was not that bad. The couple will recover. He will not have to lie to the police.* All vanquished. Now he felt his most recent belief — that, in the end, in some way he could not yet see, justice would be served – was also slipping away.

The double doors on the front of the mosque opened suddenly. A young man in a dark suit, perhaps only a teenager, propped the doors open and stood to the side. He was followed by six men carrying a pine casket. Mihran was struck by the casket's simplicity. It looked like something out of an old western, the kind of hand-made box you might see a cowboy buried in. The men eased the casket into the back of a hearse parked in front of the building, went back inside, and returned with a second casket. Soon a dozen men were gathered in small circles on the lawn. Most looked toward the ground or away when speaking. A few appeared to be crying. If any women had attended the services, they remained inside or had exited through another door. Except for the absence of women, the gathering looked to Mihran like the Christian funerals he had attended, an observation that brought with it a twinge of shame. What would he expect at any funeral except the grieving and sorrow that was apparent to him even at this distance?

Slowly the men made their way to their cars and, along with the two hearses carrying the caskets, drove away. Mihran considered his options. Following the procession did not feel right. But he also had not satisfied whatever need it was that had brought him here. He turned the car around and headed in the opposite direction.

He drove aimlessly for a while, more or less in the direction of Armenian Town. When he turned down Inyo Street, Mihran found himself looking up at the Pilgrim Armenian Congregational Church. Every Armenian in Fresno knew the history of the building. With no place of their own to worship, the first Armenians in the valley chose to attend what was then known as the Pilgrim Congregational Church. They were allowed inside but were forced to sit in the back where there were no Bibles and no hymnals. After a nasty incident in which a late-arriving Armenian attempted to sit in another section, all Armenians were banned. A few decades later, a group of Armenians bought the building and renamed it. His Uncle Henry, among others, never tired of telling the story.

Mihran parked his car next to the church. He had no destination in mind, but the impulse that had taken him this far now compelled him to travel away from Armenian Town, away from downtown Fresno. He got out of the car and started walking. He kept his focus on the ground a few feet in front of him, which allowed people and buildings to slide by without recognition. Each step led to another, and he soon fell into an intoxicating rhythm. At some point he became vaguely aware that a considerable amount of time must have passed, but he had no idea how much. He found himself walking through vineyards and cotton fields on the edge of a narrow road. Then he was trudging on nothing more than a dusty unpaved lane. There were no trees and no shade anywhere. No shelter from the searing afternoon heat.

He began to feel dizzy. He had left the house without eating that morning, and he had not had anything to drink in a long while. His cotton shirt, wet with perspiration, clung to his skin. He could feel blisters forming on his feet. Still, Mihran kept walking. He was traveling without direction, but, he sensed, not without purpose. Although he had not seen another person in a long time, Mihran had a feeling that he was not alone. An ill-defined sensation suggested he was moving among a larger group on his otherwise solitary trek.

For no reason he could explain, he experienced a sudden urge to glance to his right. There, at the end of a row of grapevines, he saw a patch of green. He headed down the row and soon found himself at the edge of the Ararat Cemetery. He paused for a second before stepping onto the grounds, where he was instantly rewarded by the cooler air rising from the grass beneath him.

The cemetery was empty. He wandered among the familiar tombstones. When he was a child, his parents had forced him to attend every funeral held at Ararat Cemetery. Only once had he refused to go. Parnag Dikmakian had lived to be 90 and never learned more than a dozen words of English. Mihran had never once spoken with the man. What would be the point of attending his funeral? But his mother had prevailed. "It's not about you," Tarvez had explained. "Someday people you never talked to will attend your funeral."

He kept walking to the far side of the cemetery, finally stopping when he reached the Reverend Papazian stone. He could not recall who had first shown him the memorial, but he would always remember his reaction. He was no more than six or seven, and it was his first awareness that being Armenian carried with it a sad heritage. Like others who experienced this same insight, it changed forever the way he thought about himself. Mihran positioned himself directly in front of the memorial and slowly read the words:

Here Lie the Remains
Of An Unknown Armenian
Martyred By The Turks
With Million & A Half Others
1915 - 1918

These Remains Were Brought By
Rev. M. G. Papazian from Der Zore, Syria, 1930.

A million and a half others. An unimaginable number. And yet, he now knew, the actual figure could be even higher. He had heard the stories all his life. That his mother had endured and survived the horrors of that time and place was almost beyond comprehension.

Once again, Mihran had the feeling that he was not alone. Even before he looked over his shoulder, he knew what he would find. They made themselves known one at a time. The first was an elderly man, bent at the waist, dressed in a red silk shirt. His eyes were fixed calmly on Mihran. Then some young women. Two, three, four of them. In white dresses stained with the copper-red dust of the desert. Colorful scarfs kept their hair in place. All were toting cloth bags, one leaned on a walking stick. And then the children. Infants that needed to be carried and the older ones lagging behind their mothers. They all seemed to be watching him. Watching and waiting. They were, he realized at that moment, his inescapable legacy.

Chapter Thirty-Eight

The plan was to talk. To listen, really. To see whether Mihran could say the one thing, could provide the one missing piece of information that would help her make sense of everything. A largely sleepless night had left Teresa lightheaded and slightly disoriented. She forced herself to concentrate on the road. She would catch him early. Before he went to classes. They could talk outside. Perhaps go for a walk.

She parked in front of the house and reminded herself not to get lost in a tangle of arguments and irrelevant issues. She no longer knew what she wanted Mihran to do or say about Arak and the accident. She knew only that she needed assurance that she had not been wrong about him. Something that would allow her to believe again. To trust again. The depth of these needs took her to the front door and allowed her to knock three times with something approaching courage. But her resolve quickly disappeared when Tarvez answered instead of Mihran.

"Good morning, dear. Was Mihran expecting you? I'm afraid he's already gone."

"I'm sorry," Teresa said. "I thought he didn't have class until this afternoon. Did he say when he'd be back?"

"He didn't say." Tarvez opened the door as wide as it would go. "But why don't you come in and wait?"

"I should be going. I just thought I might catch him."

"It must be important if you came all this way this early in the morning," Tarvez said. "Besides, we can chat while you wait. I'd like that."

The invitation was too heartfelt to resist. "That would be nice."

185

Tarvez offered breakfast, which Teresa had already eaten, and tea, which she eagerly accepted.

The kitchen was full of the warm smells of morning. Cinnamon and sugar. Toast and jelly. And a floral scent that wafted from the amber tea that Tarvez set before her. The desperation that had driven Teresa to this place quietly evaporated.

"This is a real treat." Tarvez settled into the chair across from her. "We rarely get a chance to talk, just the two of us."

"You do seem to have a very close family."

"Some would call it a blessing."

Teresa nodded.

"And how about you?" Tarvez asked. "I don't believe you've ever mentioned any brothers or sisters."

"That's because I'm an only child," Teresa said. "Pretty unusual for a Catholic, right? I used to say I was the only only child in the parish."

"And your parents? Are they well?"

"As far as I know, they're doing fine."

"You don't stay in touch?"

Teresa bought some time by taking a slow sip of tea. "I guess you'd say my mother and I had a falling out."

"Recently?"

"When I was a girl. Thirteen, actually."

"And you never made up? In all that time?"

"Things were never the same after that," Teresa said. "We kind of came to an understanding. Eventually I moved away to college."

"Letters? Phone calls?"

"No. Not really."

"That's sad. For both of you."

"I suppose. After a while, you come to accept the situation for what it is."

Tarvez shook her head slightly, which Teresa took as a sign of sympathy.

"You know," Tarvez said, "Serena likes to call me mother. *Mayr*, actually. It's not the same as hearing it from a real daughter. But I enjoy it. Perhaps someday you might do the same."

"That's kind of rushing things, isn't it?" Teresa was caught a little off guard by the suggestion. "You know, we're not at that point yet. And we're not planning to make an announcement any time soon."

"I understand. But perhaps someday."

"The truth is," Teresa said, "I've not thought of myself as some-one's daughter for a long time."

"Can I tell you a story?" Tarvez asked.

"Certainly."

"Did you know that I once had a daughter of my own? Did Mihran ever tell you that?"

Teresa wondered for a second if she had heard the words correctly. She had wanted this conversation for a long time, but it had always seemed so out-of-reach that she now felt unprepared for it.

"Yes," Teresa said. "He did mention that."

"Vartouhi," Tarvez said. "A beautiful girl."

Teresa held her breath.

"I also had a cousin. Her name was Sona. We took care of the sheep and the goats together. Did Mihran tell you about Sona?"

"I don't think so."

"We were pregnant at the same time." Tarvez' voice was surpris-ingly calm. She sounded like a woman at peace with her past. "Every morning before sunrise we would bundle up in layers of clothes. Then we'd lead the animals out to the grassy areas. We took our lunch with us. Some days Sona would pick a pomegranate on the way to the fields. In the afternoon, when it was hot, we'd find a shady place to sit and eat. We came home with the tips of our fingers stained red from the juice."

A dozen questions came and went, but Teresa was afraid to say anything that might interfere with the flow of the story.

"Sona had a son," Tarvez said. "Arakel. But the boy died."

"I'm very sorry to hear that."

"He was born a few weeks before my Vartouhi." Tarvez paused for a moment. "I guess you know what happened to my daughter."

Without being fully aware of what she was doing, Teresa reached across the table and gently wrapped her fingers around the woman's hand.

"I wonder sometimes," Tarvez said. "What would have happened if I also had died there in the desert. Would anyone have remembered me?"

"But you survived," Teresa said.

"I did."

"And you have a good life now."

"I do."

"But how?" The sense of urgency that had brought Teresa here returned in full force and allowed her to ask the question she had held inside since that first morning in the cemetery. "How did you do it? How does a person come back from where you were?"

Tarvez nodded as if she had expected the question. She looked directly into Teresa's eyes in a way that let her know that Tarvez understood. She saw the pain. She recognized a part of herself in Teresa. And she wanted Teresa to know that she was not alone.

"At the time, I was sure it was more than I could bear." Tarvez' eyes were suddenly less focused. She seemed to have moved from telling the story to reliving it. "Whether I lived or died was no longer important. I was beyond pain. I was empty. Without life."

Teresa could feel Tarvez' fingers twitching. She held on and waited.

"Sona did not make it," Tarvez said. "Most did not."

"I'm so sorry."

"It does seem impossible to come back from a place like that," Tarvez said. "I can't say I have the answers. I can only talk about my own experience."

"Please."

"Everything I believed in had been shattered. Of course, I knew the world was not perfect. But, I thought, God will protect me. That's what I believed. That he would look out for me, like he does for everyone who turns to him. If you don't have that, if you can't believe in something like that, the world becomes a very frightening place."

"Yes," Teresa said. "Of course."

"So I had to learn to believe again."

"You mean in God?" Teresa asked. "Is that how you did it? You put your faith back in God?"

"No," Tarvez said. "Not God. At least, not the way you probably think."

"Then what?"

"I don't quite know how to put it." Tarvez stared into her cup of tea. "Goodness, perhaps."

"But not God's goodness?"

"It could be God. For some people."

"So where does one find this goodness?"

"Everywhere," Tarvez said. "It's there with everything else. It's a part of everything."

Teresa sighed. "I'm not sure I understand."

"I'm afraid I'm not very good at explaining myself."

"No, no." Teresa learned forward and squeezed the older woman's hand. "I'm following you to a point. I want to understand. But it's not that easy for me."

Tarvez took a deep breath.

"We marched until we came to a river," Tarvez said. "That river took my daughter. It was a place to be feared. A place of pure evil. But that same river saved my life. It restored us with its water. It gave us a direction, something to follow. Without that river, there would have been no hope. Not for me, and not for the others who made it out of that desert alive."

The two women drifted into an unexpectedly calm moment of silence. The smells of the kitchen returned. Teresa became acutely aware of the hand she was holding. Thin and frail. Cracked and rough. Mature and warm.

Chapter Thirty-Nine

Henry raced to Community Hospital as soon as he heard. He thought he had prepared himself for the worst, but the scene he encountered when he stepped through the doorway stopped him. In the second bed from the door, Babeg Bedrosian was propped up into a sitting position. His eyes were closed. He was not moving. Henry took a delicate step forward. He had never seen his best friend's face so pale. A clear plastic tube attached to Babeg's nostrils delivered oxygen from a metal box that hummed beside the bed. Listless skin hung from his exposed arms and chest. Babeg's usually wild hair lay flat against the sides of his head, as if, like the figure in the bed, all spirit had been drained out of it.

Henry moved to the side of the bed. Two days earlier they had shared a meal. Babeg had done the cooking. *Luleh kebob* and eggplant. His friend had bounced around the kitchen with an endless amount of energy that surely placed him out of death's immediate reach. Yet here he was. Henry was no stranger to the sorrow that came with the passing of acquaintances and loved ones. But the realization that someone as alive as Babeg could be diminished so rapidly settled heavily on his chest.

After several quiet minutes, Henry leaned forward and, in a near-whisper, spoke softly in the direction of his friend. *"Kh'ntrem."* Please.

Babeg opened his eyes. A confused expression slowly gave way to a weak smile of recognition.

"I knew you would come." The voice was soft and raspy.

"You had another heart attack."

"A bad one."

"What do the doctors say?"

191

"Congestive heart failure," Babeg said. "At least they're not hiding anything. Heart failure. That's pretty clear."

"Are you comfortable?"

"As much as anyone has a right to expect." Babeg's eyes followed the plastic tubing that connected him to the machine next to his bed. "You know, I'm 68 years old."

"That's not so old."

"Time to start wrapping things up."

"Let's not talk about endings now."

"That's exactly what we ought to be talking about." Babeg's voice was stronger now, his eyes more focused. "That's what I've been lying here thinking about. Endings. Beginnings. And all the stuff in the middle. The whole story."

"Let's think positive," Henry said. "Let's talk about what we'll do when you get out of this hospital."

"I am thinking positive. It's a good story. It makes me happy to think about it."

"You've had a good life. With more to come."

"I'm not a rich man," Babeg said. "But I made it through. I had fun. I had a wonderful marriage. And I've got some people who care about me. What more can you want? Enough already."

"A lot of people care about you."

"You too, Henry," Babeg said. "Think about your life. If you do — if you really do — you can't help but be pleased about things."

"True enough," Henry said. "Good times and bad times."

"No, no," Babeg said. "It's all good. Even the parts we didn't like. Don't you see?"

A nurse entered the room. She checked Babeg's blood pressure and pulse, recording each reading with a noncommittal expression. The two men exchanged quiet glances.

"Could you do something for me?" Babeg asked when the nurse was gone.

"Anything."

"Could you bring me a beer?"

"I don't think the doctor would approve."

"Of course he wouldn't," Babeg said. "A bottle of beer. Just one."

"Maybe tomorrow."

"I wouldn't wait that long."

"What if we get caught?"

"What can they do? There's a liquor store practically across the street. That guy who used to work for Bakalian runs it. You know who I mean."

"You're in the hospital to get better."

"If you can't enjoy a bottle of beer with your friend, what's the point? Why hang around if you can't have a beer with a friend?"

"Nurses come in and out of here all the time."

"It is a happy story, isn't it?" Babeg said. "If that's not worth a beer, I don't know what is. That's the lesson here. That's the moral of the story. Celebrate while you can. You should do that too, Henry. Don't wait until you're like me."

Babeg lifted his right arm in Henry's direction. Despite the vitality in his voice, Babeg could raise his arm but a few inches. Henry extended his own hand to form a loose handshake. Babeg had barely enough strength to hold on. It was the grip of a dying man.

For several wordless minutes, Henry stood next to the bed holding Babeg's hand. It was time to set his own wishes aside.

"I'll be back in a few minutes," Henry said.

"You going to get that beer?"

"Two beers." Henry moved toward the door. "We're going to celebrate together."

Chapter Forty

Mihran's Saturday began with a series of surprises. Henry stopped by the house during breakfast to announce that the Saropians should go on a family picnic that afternoon. The harvest was over, he said, and the weather promised to be marvelous. A perfect time to be outside with the family. At first, neither Mihran nor his mother knew quite how to respond. The suggestion came only four days after Babeg Bedrosian's funeral, a time for somber moods and quiet activities. And then, when Mihran asked if he could invite Teresa, Henry seemed surprised by the question. By all means, he replied. It wouldn't be a family outing without her. The sequence continued when Teresa eagerly accepted the invitation. Things between them had been in flux in recent days, and an important conversation certainly was waiting somewhere down the road. But for now, he was content to move at whatever pace Teresa preferred.

As it turned out, Henry could not have picked a more beautiful afternoon. Patches of orange and gold were beginning to appear on the tallest branches in Roeding Park. The summer haze had vanished along with the heat, making the Sierras that define the eastern rim of the valley impossibly close. As always, Henry insisted on driving his Cadillac. Arak joined him up front, while Ana and Eliz rode with their mother in the spacious back seat. Mihran, Tarvez and Teresa followed in Mihran's car and watched Ana make faces at them through the back window all the way to the park.

The meal was a smaller version of the summer gatherings by the river. *Shish kabob*, wheat pilaf, *tabbouleh*, stuffed grape leaves, baklava. Henry sat at the head of the table, more interested in seeing that everyone had something to eat than in filling his own plate. Ana finished her meal quickly and entertained herself by running circles around the table. Henry joined in the fun by extending an open palm every time she passed. Ana slapped her great uncle's hand and squealed on each lap.

"Wouldn't you love to have the energy of a four-year-old?" Serena said.

"Mihran, why don't you take your niece to the play area?" Henry said. "Take her down the slide. And let her play on that thing with all the colors that spins around."

Mihran extended a hand to Ana. "What do you say? You want to go to the playground?"

The girl grabbed his hand and led the way.

"Arak, why don't you join them?" Henry said.

"Why not?" Arak pushed himself away from the table.

The brothers walked on either side of Ana. They had spoken very little since the harsh words that passed between them during their dinner with Anaforian. The girl bolted when they neared the play area. She grabbed the middle of three swings, unconcerned that the girl to her right and the boy to her left were several years older than she was.

Mihran stood behind his niece. "Need a push?"

"Watch me." Ana started pumping her legs and soon was swinging in as high an arc as the older kids. Mihran and Arak retreated to a nearby bench. Several minutes passed before Arak broke the silence.

"Teresa seems to be getting along well with everyone," he said.

"It's not easy for her. She had some problems with her own parents."

"Not a good sign."

"She likes Mom a lot," Mihran said. "And I bet she and Dad would have gotten along pretty well."

"Sounds like you're thinking about making her part of the family."

"It's hard to say. Maybe. Someday."

Ana glanced their way each time she reached a new high point. There was no mistaking the pride in her expression.

"I guess I should have expected it," Arak said.

"You have a problem with that?"

Arak didn't answer.

"What have you got against Teresa, anyway?" Mihran asked.

"You can see the Mexican in her, you know," Arak said. "In the eyes. I see it all the time on the farm."

"I would love for my children to be as attractive as Teresa."

Ana was now the only child on the swings, but she showed no sign of slowing down. Her bright orange dress billowed on each arc, and she looked to Mihran like a large golden poppy swaying in the wind.

"It's not just what they look like," Arak said. "People are different. It's in their blood. Just look at all the Mexican fruit pickers. How come none of them own anything but the rust bucket they drive from farm to farm?"

"There was a time when Armenians did that work."

"Exactly my point. Armenians used to work the farms, now we own them. How many Mexican farm owners do you know?"

"I'm sure there are lots of Mexican farm owners in Mexico."

"I'm just saying, people are different," Arak said. "You start mixing your blood with other blood, and pretty soon, what have you got?"

There was nothing to be gained by continuing the discussion. Mihran turned his attention back to the play area, hoping to steer the conversation to something about Ana. But his niece was not on the swings. His eyes darted all around the area, pausing on each child. Nothing.

"Where's Ana?" Mihran stood to get a better look.

"Ana?" Arak was on his feet. "Where is she?"

The brothers were nearly running by the time they reached the empty swings. They dashed around in separate directions calling out the girl's name.

Ana was not in the play area.

Mihran scanned the surrounding park. The grass extended in all directions. Vast open spaces dotted with pine, palm and Eucalyptus trees, picnic tables and children playing games.

"There!" Mihran pointed to a tall man in a beige shirt a couple of hundred feet away and moving quickly. The man was carrying a child in his arms. A child in a bright orange dress.

They started running.

The man stopped next to a faded green Buick. He set the girl down but kept his arm around her while opening the passenger door.

"Stop!" Arak was within twenty yards. "Stop right there!"

The man looked their way and confirmed what Mihran had already assumed. It was Deniz Aybar.

Arak dove at Aybar, driving his shoulder into the Turk's chest and sending the two of them sprawling onto the grass. Mihran lifted Ana before the girl could comprehend what had happened. He stepped away from the Buick and turned the girl's face away from the fight. Ana's wide eyes studied Mihran's expression for clues about how she should respond. He could feel her heart pumping wildly as he pressed his niece against his chest.

Arak appeared to have the upper hand. He sat on Aybar's chest and threw fist after fist. Aybar covered his face with his arms and absorbed the blows. But the Turk had the advantage of size and, with a roar, threw Arak off him.

Aybar leapt to his feet and grabbed a fallen tree branch the size of a baseball bat. He pointed the branch menacingly at Arak. The two men stood facing each other, panting and angry.

"You killed my brother," Aybar said.

"Nobody killed your brother," Arak said. "Talk to the police. Your brother ran his goddamned car into a goddamned tree."

"You're a liar."

"You tried to hurt my girl." Arak moved right, then left, looking for an opening. "You coward. You goddamned Turkish coward."

"My brother's death must be avenged." Aybar moved in sync with Arak.

"Come after me, if you want. But never touch my family."

"You cannot stop me. You will have to kill me to stop me."

"So be it."

Arak took a step forward. Aybar swung the branch wildly. He missed once, but the second swing caught Arak in the side. Arak grabbed his ribs and doubled over. Aybar swung again, just missing Arak's head but landing a blow between the shoulders. Arak fell face-first on the grass.

Aybar looked at Mihran as if considering whether to strike another blow or to run. Mihran set Ana on the ground and took a step toward Aybar. The Turk bolted to his car and sped away.

Mihran raced to his brother, who was already pushing himself off the ground. Blood ran from a cut above one eye, and he seemed dazed. Arak stood, but he held his ribs and struggled to catch his breath. Mihran walked calmly back to Ana, who had remained quietly in the place where he had put her. She latched onto his leg. By the time Arak joined them, the focus had returned to his eyes.

"I'm going after that bastard," Arak said.

"First we're going to make sure you're OK." Mihran put his arm around Arak's shoulder.

Arak threw the arm off.

"Leave me alone," Arak shouted. "I said, I'm going after him."

"We'll call the police." Mihran lifted Ana. "They'll track him down. For God's sake, this is attempted kidnapping. He'll spend years in prison."

"No police." Arak moved as quickly as he could toward the picnic area. "This one's mine."

Even with his niece in his arms, Mihran easily kept up with his injured brother. Arak held his arm close to where he had taken the hit to the ribs. His steps were uneven, and he let out an occasional groan when his foot hit the ground.

Teresa was the first to notice their approach. She rose from the table and ran toward them.

"Good God. What happened?"

"We have to call the police," Mihran said.

Serena ran to her husband. "You're hurt. Look at you. You're bleeding."

Arak pushed her aside. He made his way to Henry's Cadillac, where he opened the door and sat behind the steering wheel.

Mihran handed Ana to Serena and raced to the car.

"What are you doing?" Mihran yelled through the open driver's side window. "You're hurt, Arak. You need to see a doctor."

"I'm going to take care of this." Arak started the engine.

"Don't be stupid." Mihran positioned himself a few feet in front of the Cadillac. He spread his arms to show he was willing to block the moving car, if that's what it took. Arak threw the car into reverse and floored the accelerator. He spun the Cadillac around and sped off.

Mihran turned to find Henry and Teresa a few feet away. Serena and Tarvez, each holding one of the girls, watched from the picnic area.

"One of the Turks," Mihran said. "One of the Turks who attacked me. He must have been following us. He tried to kidnap Ana. Arak stopped him. But he hit Arak with a branch. Hit him a couple of times pretty hard."

"Where is this Turk now?" Henry asked.

"He got in his car and drove away," Mihran said. "That's where Arak's gone. He went after him."

"I'll call the police."

Mihran knew that Teresa's eyes were locked on him.

"We can't wait for the police," he said.

Chapter Forty-One

Mihran sped down Cedar Avenue, heading north. Henry had made no effort to stop him. There was only one place Arak would know to look for Deniz Aybar. Anaforian had talked about it. Somervel's old farm. Somewhere in the northeast end of town. The Turks living in some rickety shacks once used for migrant workers. Arak had seemed to know exactly where they were.

Mihran closed his eyes at a red light and tried to recall the conversation. Anaforian and Arak had made jokes about the shacks. They laughed about a falling roof flattening the Turks. But where? Where were the shacks? Probably not too far from the college. But on what street? Somewhere in the back of his mind Mihran thought he remembered Willow. Or Peach. Or could it have been Maple?

A horn honked. The light had changed. Mihran sped away from the intersection. He decided to try Willow. It was the best he could do.

Then another image came to him. The rifle. One of two wrapped in yellow cloth. One for work, one for home. That's what Arak had said. Arak could have stopped at his house on his way to Somervel's old farm. Of course, he could have. Easily.

Mihran played out the scene in his imagination. Arak holding the rifle. Arak moving among the old migrant shacks looking for Deniz Aybar. Arak aiming the rifle.

He hoped Aybar would not be there.

***

The sensation on the side of his body was no more than a dull ache. But any movement — turning the steering wheel or even taking a deep breath — sent a bolt of pain charging through him. At least one rib was broken. Of that, Arak was certain. Other wounds — his back, his left hand, his left shoulder — made themselves known only when he paid attention to them. He would worry about all that later. He had a job to do, and no amount of pain was going to stop him.

No one would blame him for going after someone who tried to hurt his daughter. Any man worthy of being a father would do the same. The rifle, loaded and ready, sat on the passenger seat.

He tried to picture the dilapidated shacks on Somervel's old farm. He was almost certain that, at one time, you could see them from the road. But how many years ago was that? They were ready to fall down even then. It was hard to imagine anyone living there. He slowed the Cadillac. He had a sense that he was close.

Then he saw them. About fifty yards off the road, protruding from behind rows of grapevines. Four weathered structures. More the size of tool sheds than houses. Peeling paint. Boarded-up windows. Two of them leaned to one side. All of them looked abandoned.

Arak parked a few hundred yards down the street. They might be waiting for him. He grabbed the rifle and slipped quietly out of the car.

The grapevines ran parallel to the paved road. One row at a time, Arak slid under and between the unkempt vines as he made his way to the shacks. He crouched behind the last row and studied the structure directly in front of him. Dried weeds protruded from a rickety wooden porch, and the roof had been patched with a half dozen different kinds of shingles. But the glass in the front window was still intact and covered from the inside with dark curtains. Arak studied the curtains for a few minutes but saw no movement to indicate that someone inside was looking out.

He eased his way down the row to the next little house. This one seemed less livable than the first. All the windows he could see were boarded-up, and there was a hole in the wall near the front door large enough for small animals to pass through. Surely no one was living in this one.

The porch on the third house was missing, but several cardboard boxes stacked near the front door were only slightly weather-worn, suggesting that they had been sitting there no more than a few weeks. Still, the windows were boarded-up, and there was no suggestion that the shack might be inhabited. And even if people were living here, he could see no sign that they were home at the moment.

As Arak made his way toward the last building, a gleam of reflected sunlight from somewhere behind the third house caught his eye. He paused for a moment, unsure, then eased out from behind the cover of the grapevines to get a better look. Abandoned appliances and farm equipment were strewn in the open space behind the house. And next to an old washing machine and some tractor parts sat a car. Arak moved closer. It was the faded green Buick, its chrome bumper reflecting the afternoon sun.

Arak eased his way around the shack to the front of the structure. He stood to the left of the door, rifle in hand, and considered his options. If the flimsy door was unlocked, he could rush inside, rifle aimed forward. If it was locked, he could kick it in. The noise would alert anyone inside, but the rifle still gave him an edge.

As he reached for the knob, Arak heard a noise coming from behind the house. He quietly made his way to the rear of the structure. When he peered around the last corner, he saw Deniz Aybar's back. The man was leaning over the open hood of the Buick and whistling. It apparently had not occurred to Aybar that someone might be coming for him. The advantage, Arak realized, was his.

Arak glanced around. There was no one in sight. As far as he could tell, there was no one else on the property. He positioned himself about 15 feet behind Aybar. He had only to wait for the man to turn around. A shot in the back might be hard to defend. It also would not be as satisfying. He wanted Aybar to know who killed him. He wanted to watch the man die.

Arak held the rifle at shoulder level and waited. It took another minute for the Turk to turn around and discover his circumstances. He held a can of motor oil in each hand.

"Guess who's a dead man?" Arak said.

"A gun?" Aybar spoke with no hint of fear in his voice. "This is what you call a fair fight? You have a gun, and I do not?"

"If you wanted to fight fair, you wouldn't have come after my daughter. What kind of a man hurts children?"

"What kind of man kills my brother and his wife?"

"You know that's a lie."

"You know it is not. And I was not going to hurt your daughter."

"I don't believe a thing you say."

"I wanted you to know, even for a few hours, what it would feel like," Aybar said. "And then I wanted you to imagine what that loss would feel like for the rest of your life. That is what you have done to me. That is what you have done to everyone who knew and loved Emin and Hazan."

"I've never killed anyone. But this seems like a good time to start."

"You can hurt me. You can kill me. But you will pay the price. There are others who will do what has to be done. It may take a long time. But eventually you will pay."

Arak raised the rifle to eye level and aimed. "Here's the price you pay for touching my girl."

But before Arak could fire, a blow to the forehead knocked him backwards. He staggered a few steps before he realized what had happened. A can of motor oil rolled on the ground a few feet away. Arak tried to right himself and take his shot, but he was tackled by Aybar. The two men fell to the ground. Aybar landed on top, smashing Arak against the hard clay surface. The rifle went flying.

Chapter Forty-Two

Driving up and down Willow had gotten him nowhere. Now orchards and vineyards sped by on either side as Mihran raced down Peach. A series of shacks. Old and falling apart. Could he even see them from the street? He had lost a lot of time. Even if he found Somervel's farm, he might be too late.

The street veered to the left, and when he came out of the turn, Mihran saw Henry's Cadillac parked on the side of the road. There was no sign of Arak, but not far from the car stood four small weathered buildings.

Mihran parked behind the Cadillac, stepped out of the car and listened. He heard voices coming from the direction of the shacks. Men's voices. They sounded like they were shouting, but he could not make out the words. He started running.

He found Deniz Aybar and Arak squared off and throwing punches in a clearing behind one of the buildings. Arak, no doubt still hurting from the blows he had taken earlier, held his left arm protectively over his ribs. He was bleeding from the cut above his eye that he rubbed from time to time with the back of his right fist. Aybar's left eye was swollen and nearly closed. Both men were breathing heavily. They moved with a strained deliberation suggesting that they both were nearing a point of exhaustion.

Mihran watched as Aybar landed a punch to the face that sent drops of blood spraying from Arak's nose. Arak staggered backward and fell near a pile of broken concrete. His head barely missed hitting the edge of a large jagged chunk. Arak scrambled to his feet.

The scene was bloody and gruesome. But there was no gun. Mihran quickly scanned the area. He spied the rifle lying on the ground about fifty feet from where the men were fighting.

Mihran ran to the rifle. He spun toward the fighters and raised the weapon. He was about to yell for them to stop when Arak landed a hard blow to Aybar's chin. The Turk crumbled to the ground and did not move.

Arak stood over his defeated foe. Then, without taking his eyes off Aybar, he stepped toward the pile of broken concrete. Mihran watched his brother use his last bit of strength to lift a huge chunk. Arak struggled under the weight of the concrete as he lumbered toward the fallen Turk. He held the jagged chunk shoulder-high, and there was no doubt in Mihran's mind that his brother intended to drop it directly on Deniz Aybar's head. The blow would almost certainly be fatal.

"Arak," Mihran screamed. "Don't do it."

Arak glanced at his brother and seemed not at all surprised to find him here. Then he turned back to the man on the ground.

"Arak! No! Stop!"

But Arak was past listening. Nothing Mihran could say would keep his brother from completing the act.

At first Mihran was aware of nothing but the deafening ringing in his ears. Time slowed. He saw Arak's knees buckle. He saw the heavy chunk of concrete slip from Arak's fingers and start its fall. Mihran did not hear the impact. He could only watch as the sharp edge of the concrete landed on Deniz Aybar's left hand, crushing it against the hard earth.

Chapter Forty-Three

Mihran stood in the center of his mother's front yard appreciating the crisp morning air and the signs of change all around him. Fatigued maple leaves speckled the lawn. The remaining blooms on the pink and white roses that adorned the picket fence no longer demanded admiration from passersby. Beads of dew remained on shaded car windows well into the morning, and the night's chill lingered just a little longer each day.

Although eight days had passed since the shooting, the vividness of the images had not yet begun to fade. They came to Mihran in unpredictable sequences and of their own accord. Lining up the rifle sights on Arak's right leg. The chunk of concrete on the tips of his brother's fingers. Arak's foot kicking out from under him. Then the slow descent, the sharp edges of the concrete moving ever closer to the space below. He could picture Arak falling backwards. His brother holding his leg just above the ankle. Blood spilling through the fingers.

In many ways, it had been a long week. He had not gone into the office nor attended any classes since the shooting. Work was not a problem. Jack had read the account in the newspaper and graciously suggested that Mihran take some time off. Missing classes was a bigger concern. His grades would suffer, and he worried about losing the fire that had driven him to enroll less than a week after his discharge from the army. Work and college remained part of the plan, but the last time he had sat behind his cluttered office desk or had attended a class now seemed like distant memories.

In other ways, the week had contracted into the shortest possible passage of time. The race to find Arak, the fight, the rifle shot, the chaotic aftermath of ambulance and police and family and reporters all seemed to have happened within a blink of an eye. It was all so close to the moment he now occupied that Mihran could not be sure that, were he to turn around, he might not find one of the scenes still unfolding.

He had spent that first night with Teresa. They had said very little, their physical contact limited to accidental touching. They went to bed shortly after sunset, lying next to one another in the comfort of her darkened room and slipping in and out of sleep throughout the night. He went to the hospital the next morning, only to be told that Arak refused to see him. When he called Serena two days later to ask if he could visit his brother at home, she told him the time was not yet right.

The front door creaked open, and Tarvez stepped onto the porch. She was ready for church, dressed in a dark blue suit she had not worn since the cooler months of spring.

"Any breakfast for you this morning?" Tarvez asked. "We've still got a few minutes before we have to leave."

"I'm not hungry." Mihran caught the hint of disappointment in her eyes before she looked away. "But thanks."

"I wouldn't be surprised if it rained before the week was out," Tarvez said. "It would be nice to wash away some of the dust. Everything always smells so clean after the first good rain of the season."

Like everyone, she would wait until he was ready. Mihran appreciated but had not asked for this concession.

"Have you talked to Arak recently?" he asked.

"I saw him yesterday. He's getting around on crutches now. He'll probably need them for at least another week or two."

"So he's going to be OK?"

"The doctor says he'll always walk with a limp. Nothing he can do about that."

"You know he won't talk to me."

"Give him time." Tarvez started back toward the house. "Arak has always been one to hold strong beliefs. And that's good. But it sometimes takes him a while to work things through."

To Mihran's surprise, Teresa drove up. She stepped from the car wearing the green dress from the morning she almost went to church with the family.

"Room for one more?" Teresa asked.

"Seriously?" Mihran held out his hand and she took it.

"Don't over-interpret," Teresa said. "I just think this might be harder than you realize. With everyone staring and whispering. I wanted to be by your side."

"But inside the church? You sure you'll be all right?"

"We'll find out. How did you sleep?"

"Better."

"Nightmares?"

"Hard to say. More like thoughts."

"The same thoughts?"

Mihran nodded.

"Emin and Hazan?" Teresa asked.

"And their little girl."

"You know you probably saved his brother's life."

"One out of three," Mihran said. "Is that good enough? And was it even the right one?"

She allowed the comment to pass. Unfinished conversations had piled up all week.

"I've been thinking about getting my own apartment," Mihran said. "Some place out near the college."

"Really? What about your mother?"

"I've spent a lot of time trying to convince myself that she needed to have me around," Mihran said. "That I had to stay for her sake. But the truth is, I just wasn't ready."

"Ready for what?"

"A little distance. I think I need to watch things from afar for a while."

"And then what? Get your degree and move back to Armenian Town?"

Mihran stepped to the front of the lawn and surveyed the homes on the street. "You know, three houses on this block were sold in just the last six months."

"The point being that it would be easy to move back into this very neighborhood?"

"The point being that by the time I get through with college and, who knows, maybe law school, there might not be much left of Armenian Town to come back to. All three families stayed in Fresno. They just moved into nicer areas."

"Is that a good thing or a bad thing?"

"I think it's an inevitable thing."

Mihran waved to the Kirkorians getting into their car across the street. Mr. Kirkorian, nearing eighty but still driving, waved back. His wife smiled politely.

"Your mother will miss you," Teresa said.

"I'm sure I'll see her often enough."

"I hope they don't blame me for pulling you away from the family."

"I think Mom sees it the other way around," he said. "She wants to believe it's the family pulling you in."

He squeezed her hand. "She'd like that, you know."

"I do know."

The Kirkorians drove off. Soon other cars carrying couples and families passed by. Part of a procession making its way to the First Apostolic or one of the other Armenian churches in the area.

"So what about us?" Mihran asked.

"I'm here," Teresa said. "That's something, isn't it?"

"It is." He smiled. "It really is."

Tarvez stepped out of the house just as Henry's Cadillac pulled up. No one seemed surprised to see Teresa, who let go of Mihran's hand to say hello to everyone.

Mihran watched his uncle and his mother greet the woman he hoped was still his fiancé. He studied the scene as if observing from a distance. Everything about it seemed right. He was both a part of and apart from the people in his life. There are obligations one inherits. Obligations to oneself and to others. Both are important. They might even be one and the same.

Henry opened the doors of the freshly washed Cadillac and helped Tarvez and then Teresa into their respective seats. Mihran paused for a moment to appreciate the arrangement before making his way to the car. There was nothing left to do but join them.